Pieces for Small Orchestra

Lock offers fresh insight on that peculiar grief of losing someone who exists only as an idea, only in story ... The danger of stories, Lock implies, is that their very unreality can compound rather than make sense of loss.

—*Rain Taxi*

Praise for Norman Lock

Wise up and get all you can of Lock. His writing was written by a writer exquisite in the singularity (read for this "genius") of his utterance.

—Gordon Lish

[Lock's] prose is melodial, and alert to every signal from the unseen.

—Gary Lutz

Lock channels ... our gorgeous desolation, our longing for connection, both earthly and divine.

—Dawn Raffel

All hail Lock, whose narrative soul sings fairy tales, whose language is glass.

—Kate Bernheimer

... gradually the shimmer of the words deepens into a more visceral sense of menace. If Ionesco had written an American suspense thriller, it might be something like this.

—*Los Angeles Times*

Once again, Mr. Lock presents the impossible in a way that makes splendor common.

—Deron Bauman

Also by Norman Lock

Fiction

A History of the Imagination
Trio
Notes to 'The Book of Supplemental Diagrams for
Marco Knauff's Universe'
Land of the Snow Men
The Long Rowing Unto Morning
The King of Sweden
Shadowplay
Grim Tales

Stage Plays

Water Music
Favorite Sports of the Martyrs
The House of Correction*
The Contract
Mounting Panic
The Sinking Houses*
The Book of Stains*

*Published in Three Plays

Radio Plays

Women in Hiding
The Shining Man*
The Primate House
Money, Power & Greed

*Published in Two Plays for Radio

Poetry

Cirque du Calder

Film

The Body Shop

PIECES FOR SMALL ORCHESTRA
& OTHER FICTIONS

NORMAN LOCK

SPUYTEN DUYVIL
New York City

ACKNOWLEDGMENTS

The epigraph first appeared in *Fairy Tale Review* and was later included in *Trio*, published by Triple Press, and in *Grim Tales* by Mud Luscious Press.

Chapters of *A Swan Boat on the Nile* were published in *Sleeping Fish* and in *Rampike*.

"The Transformation of Alessandro Comi" was published by *New England Review*.

Pieces for Small Orchestra have appeared in: *5_trope*, *Anemone Sidecar*, *The Café Irreal*, *Connecticut Review*, *Denver Quarterly*, *Elimae*, *Filter*, *Green Mountains Review*, *Guernica*, *JMWW*, *Louis Liard* (Bordeaux), *Mad Hatter's Review*, *New!* (Paris), *Pindeldyboz*, *Rampike* (Canada), *Score*, *Sleeping Fish*, *Unsaid*, and *Upstairs at Duroc* (Paris).

Some "Pieces" were eliminated from the final work for reasons of length and narrative pace. Nonetheless, the author wishes to thank the following publications in which they appeared: *Harp & Altar*, *Knock*, *The Salt River Review*, and *Snow Monkey*.

"To Each According to His Sentence" was published in *Gargoyle*.

The author is grateful to the National Endowment for the Arts for its award of a fellowship in 2011, which enabled him to complete this work.

Library of Congress Cataloging-in-Publication Data

Lock, Norman, 1950-
Pieces for small orchestra & other fictions / Norman Lock.
p. cm.
ISBN 978-1-933132-85-3
I. Title.
PS3562.O218P54 2011
813'.54--dc22
2011012429

CONTENTS

For R.M. Berry, Brian Evenson,
Karl E. Jirgens, Eugene Lim,
Gordon Lish, and Faruk Ulay

He was one who was writing a book of tales. In the middle of his book, he left a note in which he confessed to all things—no matter how wicked or shameless—that were set down in the book, like fiction. In it he mentioned lightly, as if wanting it to be overlooked, that at the end of his writing of this book he would write another, his last, in which he would disappear forever in a manner to be decided later.

A SWAN BOAT ON THE NILE

Literature is a simple game I made up in the dark.
Raymond Queneau

1.

The boat was wrecked and slid into the sea, its single stack hissing briefly like a cigar thrown into the water, its little red light put out. A rock had jumped up out of nothing, though it seemed as if we had struck a piece of solid night, so very black it was and indistinguishable from the water and the night sky, too. It might have been night itself and not granite on which the ship foundered. Dressed only in pajamas and slippers, I had come out on deck to lean against the rail and smoke because of the heat in the cabin and my anxiety. I went over the side— my dispatches left behind me to sink with the rest. I did not drown. Uncannily the sea upheld me. I ought to have drowned with the others, but a wave bore me up and, after a time, discharged me in shallows whose blackness was absolute, holding not so much as a particle of moon or star light. Scarcely had I been aware of myself, carried landward by an obliging tide. I might have slept. It might have been sleep that kept me from drowning. I woke on the beach with the morning light, next to the captain's boat-shaped hat. I woke although there was no evidence that I had been asleep. If I did wake—into what did I wake? Unless I am sleeping still.

2.

On the beach, a bear was setting out folding canvas chairs. His striped jersey was faded by the sun. I spoke to him shyly as anyone would with only slight acquaintance of bears. His replies were intelligible. He appeared to be well on in years but was, nevertheless, robust. He handled the chairs effortlessly. To my question whether the place where I had washed up was an island, he declared it to be so. "Large or small?" "Quite small," he said. He then tried to sell me a ride on a swan boat, which at that moment was straining to be away with the tide. "You can circle the island in no time," he said, drinking beef-tea from a glass. I wanted nothing to do with boats of any description and told him so. He shrugged. "Are you a man dressed like a bear or a bear that can talk?" I asked, angered by his indifference. He did not deign to answer. "Are there women on this island?" I asked him next although I was not convinced that it was an island. "Yes!" he leered shamelessly. I thought then that a bear dressed in a man's clothes was undignified and unworthy of a higher animal. If he was a bear. "At this hour, they are all in their beds." I pressed him to tell me where. The beach was empty except for the hut in which the canvas chairs had been stored for the night and a forest of pine trees, each tree standing close to the one next to it. But having withdrawn into taciturnity, the bear would say no more—not on this or any other subject I put to him. If it was a bear and not a man masquerading as one. Though what might persuade a man to dress as a bear in so sultry a climate, I could not guess. Unless he was made to submit for reason or reasons unknown.

3.

The ways into the forest were without number. I entered as if through a door, which opened and closed behind me. Immediately I was seized by shadows—those sinister orderlies of night—and beaten. They spoke Dutch or a language like it, each word a stone that, falling one on top of another, raised walls in the twilight as if to entomb me. Bleeding, I pinched my nostrils to staunch the issue, which tasted of rust and salt. My hand smelled of pitch. Astringent, it brought me to myself again. The walls dissolved, tumbling down in an avalanche of stones, while the ruffians, dropping their sticks, slipped away. I might have imagined them because of my terror to be without map or compass here in the uncertain light. They were useless where they lay on the bottom of a sea that might have been the Tyrrhenian, for I had embarked at Naples on a diplomatic mission to Benghazi. I began now to be hungry and would have despaired had a sandwich wrapped in wax-paper not caught my eye and, next to it, a carafe of sweet water. I refreshed myself, hearing in the distance all the while a groaning, neither human nor animal, but what a tree might make put to the rack. The sound came from far away and joined with others in a difficult counterpoint woven on the loom of the crowding trees: the laughter of women, there was, and also a bell's voice—not that of the deeply sonorous bell tolling in a cathedral tower but a small, nervous one. I thought that the women must be those who had been asleep when I arrived this morning on the beach in thrall to strange dreams, but what the bell might signify I could not tell. I stayed a long time in the forest, hardly daring to move, while the twilight gave way to darkness and that to daylight or what portion sifted through the high leaves to the roots and creepers that tried to ensnare me. From gas jets in the branches, sickly greenish blooms of light trembled. My fancy, ordinarily dull and insipid, was sharpened to a degree I had known before only in fever. Recalling the bear lolling on a canvas chair, I wondered if I might not be inside a delusion and not on an island at all, if island it was. Far away the wood suffered, a bell told by its sound that it was moving, and women laughed. What quality of laughter, what meaning it held for me, was impossible to divine. I wanted to find them—this, I did know—but the trees jostling one against another would not let me walk farther on—no, not even crabwise—and already another night was falling. I would have to go back to the beach. I considered that, in dreams, one does not go back. One is only and always thrown headlong into darkness. Doubting that this was a dream induced by fever or some other cause, I was afraid.

4.

The beach chairs were all put away. The attendant man or animal was gone. Where all had been utter blackness the night of my arrival (how many days past?), the beach now shone; the shallows and gullies were agitated by celestial light. I was able to study the footprints in the neighborhood of the hut but could deduce nothing from them: they had been made by ordinary shoes and sunk in the night-clotted sand to a depth that could have been made either by man or beast. Only then it was that I wondered to what use the folding chairs were put, for the place appeared to be deserted. Perhaps they served as an occupation for the attendant, who, otherwise, would fall into sickness or despondency; perhaps they survived as something merely habitual but nevertheless necessary. I walked to the reach to the right of the hut, returned to it, and followed the same procedure in the contrary direction. In this way I was able to verify my impression of a general desertion. Only the hut intimated a settlement—that and, in a cove or narrow estuary, the swan boat bleached in the absence of all light but what was coolly shed by the moon and—less significantly—the stars. The swan boat would have set out on its own for the interior if the mooring line had not been fixed, presumably by the attendant. Of course, the beach might have been peopled, even thronged, during the interval when the shadows were at their most circumspect; I mean to say from late morning until late afternoon—times of day in which I had been elsewhere. But I doubted it for reasons other than the footprints cast in the sand, belonging, as I determined, to the attendant alone. Did not the chairs and the tickets wound on their fat pink roll have the look of things unused? In any case, it was not loneliness or the want of others that caused me to unfasten the rope and, taking my place on the wooden seat, ride quickly a current fed by a mysterious source into the trees. It was hunger, obscure in its origin and satisfaction. There was on the seat beside me a stereoscope, but I decided against looking into it—afraid of what I might see there. Something told me—I tell you that my instincts had been made acute!—to beware sensations whose novelty might have power to undo me.

5.

I closed my eyes in the gloomy passage, which pursued a course impossible to follow by any other means than instinct—not mine but the water's, which had observed its own imperatives in cutting wide a trench through the forest floor. Here and there an ibis or flamingo stood on the muddy margins, waiting on one leg. The swan boat appeared to know the way. Whether it was endued with intelligence or some primitive organization of desire and appeasement, I could not guess. The seat was tapestried in a depiction of a childhood scene I almost remembered. But to stare overlong at it was to fall into a lascivious contemplation never to be escaped. This, I knew as one does in dreams with the certainty of unreason. Not that I knew myself to be laboring inside a dream. Though I leaned at times toward this supposition, I had not the slightest evidence to confirm or deny it. I closed my eyes as the swan boat flew onward and recalled Werner's flight of speculation in a coffee house on the Ringstrasse. We had gone there after the premiere of Spinelli's *Waltz of the Viennese Bears*, whose adagio had caused in us a melancholy almost past enduring. Wiping a wayward drift of cream from his upper lip, Werner had declared with puzzling vehemence that a dilemma was, in fact, an ethical construct that offered no obstacle to the actualization of desire. "A decision taken is not limiting," he maintained, "because the alternative, which we consciously reject, is embraced by our animal nature. At this moment, I am eating a Napoleon as well as the Sacher torte I wished equally but abjured for appearance's sake. At this moment, I am also lying in bed with Helene, whose company by any other philosophy I should have had to forgo in order to keep yours tonight. There is no such thing as the road not taken." He lit a cigarette and went on: "We glimpse those lives lived otherwise and elsewhere, in our dreams; later, I'll see myself and Helene clasped while I am asleep to this world and awake in another." If it was as Werner said, might I, in fact, be on the steamboat crossing the

Tyrrhenian to Benghazi instead of on a swan boat—or,
rather, on them both at once?

6.

Disquieted by dreams, I went up on deck and, leaning
against the rail, studied the moon's parenthesis hanging
in the west. My cigar's smoke lost itself in the ship's own,
which mingled its black particles with the blacker ones of
night. Blacker still was the sea, which invisibly moved on
its great hinge. It groaned beneath the ship, or the ship
did, racked upon the sea's steely bed. I recalled another
boat—pink it was and obedient to a rush of tea-colored
water. I recalled a bear and thought it had spoken to me
in the language of men of my own country. But I soon
laid aside those memories as follies of a sleeping mind.
I turned my mind instead to Benghazi and my mission
to my countrymen there, who were competing with the
Greeks for sponges and hoping to subjugate the Libyans.
Because the plague lingered yet on the Cyrenaican coast,
I had not wanted to accept my government's commission.
But Beatrice had persuaded me that our future together
depended on the generosity of those in power. I wished
that I might be allowed to live quietly in Rome in a small
pensione close by the Tiber and paint pictures. But my
father's example and Beatrice's ambition dictated a life
of obligations and public affairs. I had not painted in
more than a year; the paints by now must be caked in
their tubes. I should like to paint *this*, I told myself—
this moon and my cigar-end's answering light among
night's black draperies. I should like to paint the captain,
who had spent his youth in the brothels of Smyrna and
Messina and would not now willingly leave *The Minos*

for fear of losing himself once more in the toils of desire. He had the look of someone who has extinguished his self's last ember. His eyes seemed to be fastened onto eternity, which is also death. I feared the plague and also the Libyans, who wished the Italians dead.

7.

On each word, I step out further into the darkness that lies at the end of all words. In this way, do I write life into being and stave off death. And so might not there be now on its way a ship of Barbary pirates set against The Minos *to plunder and scuttle it? It takes only a little imagination to see it—like a photograph in the developer bath composing itself in the outer darkness spar by mast, cabin by deck swarming with Moroccan sailors, whose hands grasp scimitars ready to hack us to pieces. Those words aforesaid—did they not assemble out of nothing a kind of life? And having done so, can it be possible to revoke, undo, and uncreate it? Or having been conjured, is it—figment or its opposite—an irrevocable fact like any other? But let it be kept for another story—that of the Barbary pirates, one that may tell itself in a slowly unfurling dream. For words want to speak now of my arrival in Libya.*

8.

Steam as if all spent, our ship staggered between enormous lions rampant in stone at the entrance to Benghazi's harbor. Beyond, a broad esplanade submitted to the jurisdiction of shadows laid down by late afternoon sun. The sun was African. The frank shadows appeared incapable of deceit—unlike those that lurked with sinister intent beneath tables and in the corners of rooms where women, exhausted as gladioli by a lewd summer heat, peered without confidence in tarnished mirrors. They were gripped by a despair born of Sahara as well as plague, which neither the green mountain nor blue gulf could dispel. Like them the shadows on the esplanade, cast by arcade and fountain, were languid. But their languor did, in fact, conceal a restlessness, a malevolence waiting to be unlimbered. The water in the harbor lay flat under the sun's heavy hand, scarcely ruffled by the hot wind—no, not wind but rather fitful gusts full of heat and fret. The plague festered beneath floating scarves of smoke compounded of hashish, incense, and tobacco. I walked through the arcade as if waiting for my throat to be cut, though I knew the plague (gorgeous as a freshet of blood) killed with deliberation. Already, *The Minos* was steaming past the lions to escape quarantine. I looked for a conveyance to take me to the offices of the Italian legation but could find none. All life might have been extinguished, so desolate the streets and alleys, so absent were they even of sounds betraying a human or animal presence. There was about them the absolute stillness of the slaughterhouse at the end of the day. The ship was far out on the Gulf of Sidra, and I wished myself on it. But inside my briefcase were letters for the Italian consul.

9.

Would I have recognized my divided self on its various ways if Werner had not entertained me that night on the Ringstrasse with his fantastic conceit? Before it, I had been as one embarked with the glass trained on the sea ahead—too entranced by future prospects (no matter

how changeable) to look backward or to left or right.
Had I done so—to continue the figure—would I have seen
myself conducting myself in ways that would make me a
stranger to myself? A man on a swan boat conveying me
beneath the trees toward an interior. There was about the
excursion that much reality, though the direction of the
current seemed to violate hydrological principles as they
applied to this earth—mine and yours. The swan boat
was worn (I had not noticed it) with, here and there, its
pink paint chipped to reveal the raw wood. I do not think
a swan boat in a dream would look so battered and worn!
And are Beatrice and my father not themselves figures
in an itinerary, neither more nor less strange than any
other? And does not their palpable reality confirm that of
the swan boat and the steamship bound for their separate
destinations? (That they will one day encounter each
another is no more unlikely than likely a happenstance. I
foresee nothing! I simply follow—let me call it an epical
impulse.) No, I was not sick or mad or in the midst of
a delirium. It was—all of it—true. These itineraries are
records of accidents that befall an irresolute mind. That
of a man who does not know his mind—or knows it too
well, every twist and pathway, and cannot keep to one
alone.

10.

From the roof of the legation, I could see the steamship
and on its deck a heliograph flash in the setting sun its
illegible messages. That instrument was none other than
my monocle's polished lens. I was leaning against the
deck rail while standing in Benghazi beside a Venetian
girl, who had escorted me to the rooftop to view the city.

Despite the distance, I saw how—at one and the same moment—I looked from the deck toward the tall building near the dock and from it to *The Minos*. I almost called out to Werner, wishing to report this irrefutable proof of his conjecture. But I feared to find myself again on the Ringstrasse and doubted that the mind could withstand an infinitely propagating story. So I rid mine temporarily of Werner and also of my shipbound self, concentrating on the young woman. She possessed the enchantments of her kind—a lyrical figure and dark eyes too deep to sound. She felt it necessary to justify the absence of Libyans in the streets by reason of the plague as if I were a foreign dignitary liable to be offended instead of a minor legate of a hostile power. "Many have fled," she said, "and those who could not leave are hiding indoors." Suddenly I was embarrassed by the insignificance of my mission: to resolve a territorial dispute over sponges! I had allowed myself to be cajoled. I had indulged my vanity with the idea of being an envoy. I had bought a silk hat and affected a monocle, which was winking conspiratorially at me now from the horizon of the Gulf of Sidra! I staggered under the weight of my folly. My eyes stung, and the light went out. I would have swooned, had Claudia not taken my arm. "Forgive me," I said. "A sudden weakness." She led me from the roof, down the stairwell, and out onto the street. "There is a *trattoria*, which has not closed," she said. Thinking not at all of sponges, I allowed her to guide me through the streets, which under the severity of that late sun groveled beneath our feet, toward a cellar fragrant with oregano and coffee.

11.

A thought once entertained—no matter how briefly or how we might repent of it—cannot be rescinded or annulled. *This is one of the game's imperatives!* In Benghazi I had wished, momentarily, to speak to Werner. Having wished it, there was nothing that could prevent the wish's actualization. It matters not at all that Werner was dead and that we had been together last, in Vienna the year before. *My stories ravel like strands of vermicelli on a plate—coiling, turning back on themselves, falling one across the other.* And because he could not go to Benghazi (this story with its complex reticulation is mine, not his), I went again to Vienna. "Went" is incorrect inasmuch as it asserts a movement from one place to another, which was not the case. That is to say, "went" implies a presence acceding to an absence and vice versa. When I found myself with Werner in the coffee house, no such alteration had occurred: I had been with him all the while I was on a rooftop in Benghazi and aboard ship heading toward the Mediterranean. "I saw myself looking at myself," I told him. "I had been on the horns of a dilemma—my duty as an envoy to Libya and my fear of the plague." Werner looked at me as if I were mad. I was wise not to have mentioned the swan boat. It was a chimera out of place in even the fantastic aspects of my narrative. "Perhaps it is that we cannot endure having only one life," I continued. I no longer feared my mind's overthrow, not now that my lips were burning with fiery *impepata di cozze* and imagined kisses! "Tomorrow I intend to visit the *Friedhof der Namenlosen*," said Werner. "A suicide fished out of the Danube was recently interred there. I would welcome your company. Afterwards, I should like to look at the bears to see what it was that inspired Spinelli." I promised to go, for I had reasons of my own to be curious about bears, notwithstanding my conviction that a man had sold me a ticket for the swan boat. "And now I feel a visit to Frau Wolf's near the Imperial Palace is very much in order," said Werner, daubing with a damask napkin his Crown Prince Rudolf moustache. "Will you go?" I would not, being at that moment in the arms of the pretty Venetian. I might survive the knowledge that I had more than one life to traverse, but I knew myself incapable of satisfying two women at once.

12.

It was to the swan boat, however, that I woke. *To say "woke" suggests that I slept through every itinerary except that in which I was most urgently engaged. Such a supposition is, however, a convenience merely.* The swan boat glided between steep banks, rattling reeds which stuck up stiffly from the shallows. The heat was intolerable, the air pestilential. Then, I saw a thing upon the sinister bank that resembled a life-sized artist's mannequin. I mean the stilted way it walked and the wooden expression it wore. I did not consider it remarkable. How should I, who rode a swan boat down a winding channel—in my pajamas!— that seemed without end or issue, do so? I had come to think of myself (my selves) as though acting on a stage in Vienna, Benghazi, on the Mediterranean Sea, and, little by little, in a *pensione* by the Tiber—each framed by an ornate proscenium arch suitable to the prevailing taste. I turned to speak to the mannequin, but it had gone behind a sort of column raised against the sky. I should like to have inquired where the swan boat was carrying me and what else the mannequin knew of the geography of the island, if it was an island. I might have asked it, as well, about the man who sold me the ticket: whether he might not have been a bear after all. "I pity Vienna's poor bears," said Werner.

13.

Like an ox staggered by the sledgehammer, I reeled to see Werner walking down a flight of steps laid into the stream's high bank. A rusted metal sign, raised above the top step in an arch, announced: *Friedhof der Namenlosen*, Cemetery of the Unknowns. He scraped the soles of his boots clean of mud on a metal blade installed at the foot of the stairs for the purpose. "I pity Vienna's poor bears more than these nameless humans: their agony is finished." In a zoo, which assembled in minute detail around us, a bear groaned—a noise like wood splintering—and dropped down onto its forepaws to pace once more the narrow cage. In an otherwise immaculate sky, large clouds herded behind the black-iron railings of the Tiergarten Schönbrunn while a swan drew from the placid water a single lengthening strand. The moment in the Tiergarten was comprised of two antithetical states of mind: a swan boat halted on its journey and an exhibition of caged bears in Vienna's zoo. I say states *of mind* because nothing existed apart from the thought of them. What I seemed to see there was both marvelous and disquieting, like one of those spurious photographs of fairies—a cunning imposture made by exposing the same photographic negative twice. For the space of that momentary disquiet, two realities (if they may be called that) composed themselves as one at the back of my eyes, or in my mind's eye—it is impossible for me to say where the trick was done. If trick it was. Might not it have been a momentary suspension such as happens when milk is drizzled into tea before the teaspoon uniformly disperses it? I am groping, but how else can so original a sensation be explained if not by a groping after comparisons, which may be wide of the mark? The composite image (to resort once more to photography) was accompanied by an auditory simultaneity. I heard the anguished bear and the swan boat rustling among the reeds while Werner's voice floated above the scene. "How is business, by the way? Does it flourish?" I told him it did not and knew that it would not ever. My father had arranged for me a sales position in Vienna with an Italian manufacturer of printing presses. I possessed neither aptitude nor interest and knew that my ignominious return to Naples was inevitable. "How long before you go back to Italy?" I shrugged. I would remain in Vienna for six months more, enjoy the favor of two Austrian women, both hysterics, and on a rainy November afternoon accompany Werner to a cemetery and watch with mixed emotion his interment—another suicide in an age of desperate men. "I think I shall miss you, Alessandro." And I, you. "In Benghazi I thought of you," I told him, "while eating mussels." He looked at me in surprise. "I didn't know you had ever been in Benghazi!" I told him that I would be, in time, and also on a steamship menaced by pirates off the Barbary coast. He laughed and offered me a cigar. "You are a strange one, Alessandro!" Why I had been granted insight into the multifariousness of life I could not tell unless it was that I had nearly drowned. Perhaps

I had drowned and was already living out a dead man's destiny with the privileged knowledge said to be given only to those who no longer have any use for it.

14.

I leaned against the rail and smoked, watching the Libyan coast diminish until it was no more than a line trembling against the horizon, which in a little while engulfed it. All was now merely water with the cobalt sky of Africa ranged oppressively against it. I had with me my briefcase, a gift from Werner. I had tendered my resignation to the manufacturing concern and, though I preferred Vienna, could not stay on without an income. Returning to Italy, I had set myself up in a studio in Rome and begun to paint but, in the end, acquiesced to my father's and Beatrice's wishes that I enter the Italian foreign service. How could I tell them that now I had also failed their expectations for my mission to Benghazi? That instead of advancing the interests of our sponge fishermen, I had run away to Egypt with the wife of a member of the Italian diplomatic mission to Libya? That I was on a ship steaming toward the Nile and—at the same time—on a swan boat traveling languidly into the interior of a country inhabited by talking bears and wooden mannequins. These alternate, however eventful, itineraries could never be divulged. *I can do so in these pages because I foresee that they will be put to the fire before any eyes but mine shall read them.* "Is it not, all of it, fantastic?" Werner remarked from the other side of the horizon where he had been laid to rest in the rain to a mournful adagio by Albinoni. "Yes," I replied. The steamer's captain, who feared land and women and had forsaken both, touched my arm with a diffidence I

18

could not then interpret. "Would it interest you to see a ship's log in which the future is already written?"

15.

Past, present, future, the possible and conditional worlds—what are they if not galleries in a museum, where one can wander at will among time's exhibits, passing easily from one to another, along corridors, up flights of stairs and down—without method or plan— spurred by obscure impulses, one's own or another's? Is this not a more fitting metaphor of time's simultaneity than Werner's "dilemma" (even should we multiple its two horns to crown an entire herd of oppositions)? Werner attributed our ability to actualize our every desire to an animal nature. The notion might solve the talking-bear / man-masquerading-as-one conundrum; I believe my fluency in time, however, has nothing to do with the deliberate embrace of questionable pleasures but rather to a disposition of time contrary to the usual experience of it. Let me try again. It is the arrangement of time within the space of all possible existences that allows me to enjoy more than one life (or—who knows?—damns me to them). I remember the morning Beatrice arrived in Rome to persuade me, by whatever means are available to a woman who does not want to suffer the embarrassment of a jilting, to leave my daubing. "What is the meaning of this?" she asked, pointing to an oil sketch showing a pink swan boat and a mannequin—the same articulated wooden model that was leaning against an upright copy of *Inferno* on my desk. "I saw it in a dream," I said. What else could I have said? Beatrice was dazzling in the strong Roman sunlight, which was glinting from a silver necklace round her delicate throat, the dark ends of her hair, and on the Tiber's wind-beaten waves. "You must come home," she said. "Your father has begged a favor from the Minister: a diplomatic mission to North Africa. If you succeed, your future—ours—is assured. Are you going to make me beg, Alessandro?" She drew the long pin from her hat, removed the hat and shook out her hair, which tumbled—a dark and fragrant avalanche— onto her blouse. She waited for me to speak and, seeing that I did not, began to undo the buttons of her blouse, whose alternating stripes of cream and russet silk were deformed by the ample breasts beneath. She paused at the button that would relieve the tautness of the silk, with— doubtless—an accompanying sigh indicative of the relaxation of desire's prohibition, which once before I had heard escape her lips—in an olive grove above the river Po. I hear it again in the eternal present at Benghazi when I kiss Claudia and taste on her peppery lips the *impepata di cozze*, which we ate while the sun left the sky suddenly and the wind, rising, beat the gulf's darkening water to foam. "And this man wearing a bear costume—

16.

—why do you waste your time on such silliness?" Beatrice demanded. I was standing at the window with its view of black sky and of stars repeated against the blacker water by the trembling lights of the fishermen. "What makes you think it's a man and not a bear?" I waited expectantly for her answer. She sneered, "Would a bear be lying on a canvas chair?" I turned and would have questioned her further if she had not become, like cigar smoke, insubstantial—a slowly disintegrating shape in the air. "What are you talking about, Alessandro?" Beatrice, standing a moment before in the Roman light with blouse half opened, had been replaced by Claudia in her room above the harbor, invaded by the African night. And I—I was common to both and to more besides. "I am leaving Benghazi tomorrow," said Claudia as I undid the last buttons. "Where?" I asked. "Egypt." I laid her down on the bed. "Why not go by boat?" I said, my mouth in her hair, whose perfume I almost recognized. "Yours was the last," she said, "before the quarantine." Frightened, I returned to the window and looked once more at the sky and the blacker night of water spread beneath it. And as I looked, I seemed to see the Tiber and the nameless path the sea cut through the country where I had been or would be or am being washed ashore, a shipwreck. *Do you not realize yet that time is a vibration in space, commingling what is or was with what will be?* "Will you stay or go?" Her voice sounded as though it were coming from far away, as if she had begun already her journey, if only that one each makes at night during the long, absent hours. "I will come with you," I answered, not daring to turn in case she, too, should have vanished.

17.

It was not love that made me hold Claudia on the narrow bed or desire, which was spent, but fear that she would become suddenly some other—*so treacherous is life under the administration of a malignant will. With these, my capricious itineraries, I hope to escape the destination decreed for me. All depends on how cogently I create— how readily I can be persuaded to accept a model of time that thwarts my inevitable progress to the grave.* I held

Claudia fast, and together we made a night journey—arriving with none of the usual difficulties of travel in Alexandria, where the great library (another of time's exemplars) held within its rooms the possibility of perfect knowledge and the fulfillment of desire. Unlike day with its transparencies and seductive vistas, night is an opaque fluid—an ink—through which we pass from one destination to another with little to distract us. It is a dark tunnel into which we enter and, after a time, debouch to find ourselves mysteriously present. *So it seems to me; so would I have it be.* We arrived in Alexandria just as the sun was climbing out of the Mediterranean, at the threshold of Lebanon. The sun spilled its fire onto the water; the wind blew up from the east, bringing with it the aromatic smell of cedar and the calls of the *muezzin* and of the bird sellers and merchants in the bazaars. Soon the sponge fishermen will push their boats out from shore, and the plague, which we had left behind us, will strike. It will strike Claudia and me, too, while this story—the one which, having begun in Benghazi, must continue in Benghazi—carries us on its own unstoppable current. From Egypt I will watch the black flowers bloom on our skins in Benghazi as we lie in Claudia's room until our bodies are carried out and thrown onto a death cart to be burned.

18.

Captain—shall I name him for verisimilitude's sake? Captain Seferiádhis led me down a narrow passageway redolent of hemp, tar, stale tobacco, and perfume. Unshaven and unkempt, he nevertheless used scent—perhaps to summon up in memory the women of the brothels he frequented in his youth. He feared them now and, having distilled desire to this single olfactory sensation, was able to suffer his pelagic exile in tranquility. He lit a cigar and, lumbering contrary to his ship's sudden heave, fell heavily against a bulkhead. "He looks like a bear," I told myself, "dressed like a man smoking a cigar." Seferiádhis answered, "Or a man etcetera." I said nothing, unsure if it was the captain's or some other's voice that I had heard—my own, perhaps, sounding inside my head. He invited me inside his cabin, his hand describing a florid figure in the air as a seventeenth-century courtier might have done. He bade me sit in the small room's only chair while he brought from the shelf above his berth a book on whose cover was written in India ink: *Log of 'The Minos'*. Setting it before me, he opened to a page marked by a metal ruler and invited me to read the entry: "16 January, 1885. Arrived in Benghazi in late afternoon. Neither took on passengers nor discharged the ship's sole passenger—an Italian government minor official, who chose, prudently, not to land because of the plague that had broken out there. Immediately I turned the ship 'round and, entering the Mediterranean, set a course for Alexandria, arriving there at dawn on the following day." I looked up at the captain, who was standing behind me. "We have not yet reached Alexandria," I said. "It is, as I said, a log where the future is already written," he replied. I turned to a page much farther on in the book. (I had not at first noticed how voluminous it was.) "22 April, 1915. Boarded at sea by a German naval patrol near Patmos. The ship was searched and Captain Mátsas taken off under guard.—Míltos Antoníou, First Mate." I looked at Seferiádhis. "But I thought you were *The Minos*'s captain!" My monocle fell to the end of its tether in my surprise. He shrugged. "She will have others." I made to turn next to the log's last page when my hand was stayed by Seferiádhis's. "It is better not to know the end," he said. His face seemed like a worn statue's—of a gryphon or something equally fabulous and oracular. "Have you looked at it?" He did not answer. Then I turned to "15 January, 1885"—the day prior to the entry I first had read aloud. The page was empty as were all others dated before it. "The past vanishes," said Seferiádhis. "This book concerns itself only with the future."

19.

In Alexandria I saw—wandering among the tombs, the date palms, the houses on the hill overlooking the canal and the painted sailboats drawn up on its bank—Claudia and that other self of mine in pursuit of their own story's end, not knowing that it has none. That unlike *The Minos*'s log this—their book and mine—has no final entry, because time, the motive of all our lives, is a labyrinth: inside its uncounted chambers what appears to be a wall may be a turning that leads one farther on, or back, or to an annex, attic, or a walled and ruined garden forgotten even by the oldest chamberlain. I said "unlike *The Minos*'s log," but each time I visited Captain Seferiádhis's cabin and sat over his book, it seemed to have grown by an increase in pages as though the future was constantly writing itself there and that what I had mistaken for a final entry was only the latest in a record that may or may not be endless. Helpless to resist, I followed Claudia and my other self into the library's anteroom. But I went no farther, afraid of the outcome of such an extraordinary convergence.

My briefcase hanging like an impossible weight from my arm, I watched the high bronze door open and then close heavily behind them. Having nothing more to keep me in Alexandria, I returned to *The Minos* and a nearly overmastering desire to know its future.

20.

I seemed to see him everywhere: lurking in a belvedere high above the estuary, in the mobbed bazaars, in the necropolis to whose narrow, shaded paths Claudia and I resorted in order to escape beggars and sunlight—both of them ubiquitous and importunate. He was clutching, still, our leather case where commissions waited in vain to be fulfilled. *"He" is a pronominal convenience, another aspect of "I." They differ only in their realization of the possibilities contained within a single life, which is also mine as I write these accumulating sentences— possibilities thought to have been mutually exclusive.* Only in Alexandria's immense library was I free of him and his constant surveillance. Why he did not follow Claudia and me into the library, I do not know. Perhaps he chose at that moment to obey some contrary impulse or, having tired suddenly of the chase, withdrew to find a place where he might be refreshed. Whatever the cause of his retreat, I was relieved. *To split him in two so that he might retreat and, at the same time, continue his pursuit inside the library is a madness I—Alessandro Comi, author of these itineraries—refuse although such must be the case. (For so the game requires!) But lacking the omniscience of a god or narrative genius, I cannot sift my story so finely. Thus it was that I did not relate his exhortations to the sponge fishermen or his and Claudia's death agonies in a Benghazi hotel.* The marbled library was cool and restful to the eye and spirit as though it were a pool within a garden's walls, where only fitful flashes of golden carp distracted from the contemplation of serenity. *I liked to be walled up with books. I could enter one at will and lose myself among its words—it would be no easy matter, now, to find me among so many. What is even the most modest of libraries but a warren of endless and sometimes connecting passages—a mansion of rooms, each with its own furniture, guests, and time?* Shutting her eyes, Claudia permitted herself to drift off to sleep while I read a recent account of General Gordon's peril at Khartoum, in *The Pall Mall Gazette.*

21.

Like a piece of complicated music, obedient to laws of counterpoint—a braid of sound scarcely possible for ear and mind to disentangle—my stories are woven. Have you understood that each itinerary so faithfully described here is mine and that these "I"s propagated by a mind at play also belong to me? That is, they are aspects of a divisible self, bred out of my imagination for the delight of my imagination, which is as rich as my means are slender and my days numbered. My life is in danger. I am Alessandro Comi, citizen of Naples, hiding in an attic room overlooking a ruined garden, in an inglorious age, in the century that follows the events I have been setting down. Outside, enemies are hunting everywhere for such as I. I wait, and while I wait I send myself forth into the wide world: an Alessandro in Vienna, an Alessandro in Rome and in Benghazi, too, and in Alexandria— and also in a mythical country where a swan boat and a talking bear are not strange. I am in danger of losing my life and taste fear like an old coin in my mouth. The Alessandros—followers of my itineraries and characters in my stories—begin to converge in Egypt.

22.

"And this?" Beatrice next demanded of me. I studied a red-granite pillar painted the week before in oil. "It is Pompey's Pillar, part of a temple colonnade near the Arab cemetery." As an *idea* of that ancient Alexandrian column, my painting equaled it in weight and substance and—like the Colossus of Rhodes or Pharos Lighthouse, both of which exist now in thought alone—may outlive its original. I told her its history and how I had seen the ancient light of the Mediterranean fall hard upon it like a blade of chalcedony. She looked at me in amazement, believing that I had never been in Egypt. I did not bother to tell her how, on a leaden Roman afternoon, my mind will travel near to the Nile's mouth and return with images as meticulous as photographs for my hand to copy. *"Will travel," "would," "did"—tenses are meaningless when time's strict accounting is undone.* I showed her painted docks, great palaces, the Emporium, and the Apostasies. In each picture, a man and woman, minutely rendered almost to invisibility, stood in a swath of shadow. "Who are those people?" Beatrice asked. "Two who wish to hide from the pitiless sun and—equally pitiless—time, which has accumulated, hour by hour, in those stones." I did not tell her that the man in the painting is I, the woman someone loved by me elsewhere. She would have thought me mad! How much madder still, were I to tell her that she herself—I mean Beatrice—was also a figment of a mind at play or in fear of what is to come. "Won't you come back to Naples, then?" *An "I" of me will go with her, but that itinerary is another I will not relate.* She finished dressing, transfixed her hat with a long pin topped by an onyx bead, and left me to contemplate my painting of the library—outside of which a man in unblinking sunlight watched a pair of lovers pass through its high bronze doors. *I should like to be with them and become lost in literature's mazy corridors and on stairways descending to the incunabula, scrolls, and tablets of that library's antecedents burned, in brutal succession, by Julius Caesar, by Aurelian, by Theophilus's decree, and by the Muslims—making this library, Alexandria's, a palimpsest on which the writings of an ancient past are very nearly visible. Between* I should like to be *and* I am—*what a gulf is there! I put down my pen, went to the window, and, peering through the blinds, looked out onto the street where a convoy belonging to my enemy rumbled over broken cobbles on its way to war.* I put down my brush, with which I had thought to make a slight adjustment to the canvas—the addition of a flaring monocle on the pursuer's face—went to the window overlooking the Tiber, and watched as Beatrice passed on her way to the railroad station. In this life, I would not see her again. *You will not see her again.* I closed the blinds, the light jumped onto the ceiling and was extinguished there. The room returned to gloom, *and I with it.*

23.

In the time it had taken me to read some eight hundred or a thousand words and study with rapt fascination the engraving of "Chinese Gordon," as he was known since his defeat of the Taipang rebels and capture of Chanchufu, I had pictured with so vivid an imagination the rescue of the beleaguered British general as to realize it nearly in fact. All that remained to bring out Gordon Pasha, as he had been called since his destruction of the Sudanese slavers, was to find a boat willing to take me to Khartoum. Muhammad Ahmad al-Mahdi, the Sudanese zealot who had promised fire and the sword for Khartoum, Cairo, Alexandria, and Constantinople, was waiting with his army for the Nile to recede, so that it could cross the flooded ditch and complete the work of starvation, slowly reducing the town. Reading the account published in the *Pall Mall Gazette*, I had pictured myself at Gordon's side, peering at the Mahdi's tents pitched at the confluence of the Blue and White Niles through a spyglass whose lens flashed wickedly in the desert sun. I left Claudia to her dreaming *(the content of which I have not time to report)* and went along the dock in search of a ship. I was surprised to find the very one that had carried me from Naples, *The Minos*, and decided at once on her because of her name's association with the Minotaur, the labyrinth, and the judgment of the dead. I went aboard and encountered—to my dismay—my pursuer, the "I" who had refused to disembark at Benghazi because of the plague. I had imagined him in Alexandria but no longer aboard ship. Ashamed of his cowardice, which was also mine, I turned my face from his. "You!" he cried in recognition of himself.

24.

"You!" he had cried, and hearing in that single word his horror and relief to be standing finally face to face with me, I understood that ours was not a simple destiny. For myself I was pleased and repelled by him. "If you will permit me," I said, "I would like a word with you." He nodded and led me to his cabin, motioning me toward the only chair while he sat on the bunk to hear me out. I set the briefcase down between us, for it belonged to us both. "Having read this morning of Gordon's plight," I began without preamble, "I undertook to find a ship that would make at once for Khartoum to deliver him from a certain death. All day I have pictured myself in a number of *tableaux*, each more heroic than the one before. I am— let me admit it!—smitten by the idea of my famous self and see it returning to Naples with Gordon, decorated and acclaimed. I will atone for abandoning the sponge fishermen, whom I was sent to aid—." "*We* were sent," he interposed. I nodded and went on: "—for Claudia's sake." "She is a handsome woman," he said with enthusiasm. "My briefcase, with its obligation still undischarged, is a constant reproach of my dereliction." He was gratified by my frankness and resolved to return the confidence. "I played the coward's part," he said. "As a government representative, it was my duty to render assistance to my plague-stricken countrymen. Such fame as you describe will also expiate my disgrace in having refused to disembark at Benghazi." I continued for us both: "We can make amends by saving Gordon from the Mahdi. It will be splendid—we will be splendid! Ten columns and an engraving of the two of us in *The Pall Mall Gazette* and *l Giornale di Napoli*!" He agreed that it would be the making of us both. "If we can prevail upon the captain ..." "Captain Seferiádhis can be persuaded," he said. "He is a man for whom only the future exists."

25.

It was the future that made Captain Seferiádhis difficult to persuade. He appeared not at all surprised to see that there were two of us. Perhaps he thought us twins. We did not bother to explain that we were one man's two contingent selves, which by an accident of history and metaphysics had conjoined here in Alexandria. It would have delayed our embarkation. Time, we knew, was against us if we were to rescue Gordon from the Mahdi and ourselves from infamy. But the captain was in no hurry to depart. For him the future had already happened; it was written in *The Minos*'s log and could not be altered. *I, Alessandro Comi—author of these eventful itineraries— would prove him wrong, in part. My life, however, will be another story; its denouement beyond the pages of this, my book.* The captain bade us sit and, opening the log to an entry made on 28 January, 1885, read: "Stopping at the Bend of the Nile to take on fuel, we learned of Khartoum's fall two days earlier and of Gordon's death. Our rescue mission having failed, *The Minos* turned and headed north for Cairo." Seferiádhis closed the log and said, "So you see, gentlemen, there is no point in going. The trip is long and difficult; six cataracts lie between here and Khartoum, and I have little patience with the 'cataract men,' whom we must engage to haul the ship through them." He—I mean my other self—demurred, brilliantly: "But Captain Seferiádhis, it is impossible for us to do anything else! It is written in the logbook that we will go to the Bend of the Nile and then to Cairo!" Startled, Seferiádhis conceded that it was so. "But we will go no farther south than the Bend," he insisted. "And Gordon will be dead." "Perhaps," we answered as one.

26.

In Rome I watched the Tiber transform into that portion of the Nile above the first reach, where the river began its ascent to Africa. *The Minos* was underway, her twin screws beating water into foaming wake. On her upper deck, a bear wearing a faded jersey was setting out a pair of folding chairs for two passengers, whom I knew as well as I knew myself. Unlike them I had stayed in Rome to paint, resisting Beatrice's charms and my father's command. I would paint the Nile a blue such as might not exist in reality and the boat the color of those that ply the waters of dreams. I would paint the bear in its sailor's clothes, careless of questions of identity. Mine was an alchemical art, activated by desire and by desire transforming a world constituted of sensations. The world changed as readily as did a river when a wind, driving a cloud across the face of the sun, blew out its candles. It took but another wind for the river to catch fire again. All was teetering on a blade of impulse and caprice. Those men resting on deck chairs—their stories had converged—converged, also, with that of a painter who saw them as though a transparent fluid and not dull opacity separated one life from another. *Or as if we were together on one of August Ferdinand Möbius's curious bands, which has but a single surface for all its appearance of complexity.* I would paint the world so, for that is the truth of it. It is like the Nile itself, which flows apparently upward in defiance of logic and gravity. Overcome by a gust of emotion, I wondered at how prescient Werner had been, how extraordinary his philosophy, to have imagined—in a café on the Ringstrasse—a scarcely imaginable instrument to play the fugue of life! Opening

the window, I called to my two selves across the river—
the Tiber and the Nile: *they are the same river—one
flows into another, endlessly, on Möbius's band*. The two
men—Alessandros both—raised their heads to listen. My
voice came faintly to their ears, but nonetheless it came.
They looked over *The Minos*'s rail and saw—if only for
an instant—the towers of Rome. How immense is life
and how, at the same time, so very small! I lay down
on my bed and went with them up the river so that I—
Alessandro!—might paint a transfiguration, a raising of
the dead, an apotheosis not dreamt since ancient times. I
lit a cigar and, lying on my bed, watched its smoke trace
arabesques against the ceiling while, outside, my window
flashed a meaningless semaphore in the sun.

27.

"Strange," he said, "that two lives, until now separate,
should intersect on a ship steaming up the Nile! I could
not have imagined such a possibility." The little space
between us was occupied by our two briefcases. From
our cigar cases, each of us extracted a cigar. Together,
we lit them—I, his, and he, mine, companionably. "We
were separated by exigency and have been reunited,
finally, by it," I replied, drawing contentedly on the
fragrant Sumatra. *"I" and "he" are understood to be
conveniences of reference*. He drew likewise but coughed
on the richness of the smoke. I did not cough and could
not resist a superior look. Fortunately he did not notice;
the enterprise on which we were engaged depended on a
unity of resolve, a singleness of purpose. Already I felt
the pull of Khartoum. The sensation was not a pleasant
one as though disaster were waiting on the other side

of the Nile's Great Bend. "It is Werner's doing—this!" he said peevishly. "His damned theory! I would be in Rome, otherwise, making pictures." *You are, my friend, if only you knew it!* A faint cry caused us to lift our gazes from the contemplation of our two cigars' glowing ends to the river's farther shore. Having done so, our sight was ravished by a light flashing from a window there. A city, it looked to me like Rome; but I said nothing, feeling keenly his—and my own—bitterness. "But it was you who launched us on our present course," I remarked. "I would have been happy to stay on *The Minos*, reading the future in Seferiádhis's book. I had gotten only as far as April, 1915; and there was no end to the pages that came after that!" It was my turn to be peevish, and I glared at him. *Yes, waiting for the end is intolerable. I wonder how many more chapters will be mine to write before they drag me from my den? I should like to be that bear— would like to have been any one of them now that time is all but run out for me.* The Nile reasserted itself, and we looked at our hands again. "Did you ever dream of riding in a swan boat?" he asked shyly as would anyone who is prepared to defy death, concerning so childish a matter. "Have *you*?" I asked him warily. "I have," he answered, "though I am not certain it was a dream." Nor am I.

28.

The route by which I arrived in Egypt could not be traced on any map, any more than the course of time followed by this outlandish swan boat might be recorded in a chronology. *Excepting this one, which I write—like Scheherazade—to forestall the moment of my capture.* Both existed apart from ordinary time and a mundane topography described by circles of latitude and meridians of longitude. One might—like Verne's aeronaut—circumnavigate the earth and never see what I saw as the boat plied its imaginary waterway through a desert remarkable for gold-leafed proscenium arches casting *trompe l'oeil* shadows on the sand, ancient instruments and inscrutable machinery, creatures of no known kingdom, botanical gardens descended from Eden, kiosks papered over with sun-bleached notices in unrecognizable languages rendered in typographies never designed for the eyes of literate men. I was in a place elsewhere—or say, instead, that it had been set atop the common earth by a vast, laboring imagination, a demiurge *(ha!)*, which sought to intercalate a mythic world into our own. From the time of my shipwreck on an island, which was none, to this desert crossing on a river that seemed no more than a canal dug across a pleasure park—I was led by a superior will and purpose. I had come to think that the reason for my journey might be read inside a briefcase sunk beneath the Tyrrhenian Sea, where my original commission was being rewritten by an alien hand. Whatever it was that had decreed my itinerary, I felt myself close to its end.

29.

Inside my briefcase, these stories are converging on the Great Bend of the Nile although when I started my own journey I had no idea of its destination. I wished to conceal it from myself for the same reason that a man will not tell his wife what he knows in case she should, unwillingly, betray him to her torturers. My manuscript has fattened, feeding on an imagination desperate to make for itself a place in which to disappear when the assassins come for me with the death's head on their black lapels and signet rings. I meant to write about Moroccan pirates, their attack on The Minos off the Barbary Coast, and a career of "daubing" as brilliant as Whistler's; but I lack time to pull any more threads through the tangle of my work. It has been a game and something more, the writing of these itineraries. One remains to be told. If I can. If not, maybe it will write itself. Surely so many words as this will have an impetus of their own to go on a little while before they, too, fall silent! I had also meant to write about the forest in which my shipwrecked self was lost— to describe women who seemed almost to be sleeping, so very light was their attachment to the earth. I had seen them when, a boy, I had visited Dyrehavsbakken—an amusement park in Klampenborg, north of Copenhagen. It was there I had seen a bear dressed like a sailor and the lights among the trees, heard the tiny bells on the reins of the carrousel horses and at night the trees groan under a load of ice. The year was nearly at an end. There had been a swan boat, too, faded and peeling. I have said already what it is to write: how each sentence lights the way ahead. How words create out of silence and nothing everything we know. Last night I woke at the sound of breaking glass and felt, as anyone would, death's cold hand. Some words came to me—an elegant summation; but waking this morning, the words were gone from my head. They may have been meaningless; thoughts that come in the middle of the night often are. I wish I might smoke a last cigar. They've come, I hear their boots hammering on the stairs. Finished—into the briefcase with it all! I am he who was Alessandro Comi.

30.

The Minos lay above the Great Bend, her reflection unbroken on the water. Below her, carp rove through glassy corridors while on the muddy banks to either side of us ibis—sacred to Thoth, god of magic and writing, by whom Ra's will is translated into speech—walked together in procession. The sky was a confusion of effects: dusk, midday, and dawn commingling. Violet rags of sunset, the molten gold of afternoon, daybreak's viridian and rose vied for preeminence. It was as if time had mutinied against its own strict succession, or else the artist of the scene before us, thrice repenting of that captured light, had been nonetheless helpless to efface it. The scene had the picturesque quality of a theater set enhanced by a gilt proscenium that overarched, impossibly, the Nile. The play appeared to be a tragic farce: we had heard the news of Khartoum's overthrow, the slaughter of the Egyptians garrisoned there, and of the death of Gordon—due, all of it, to a grievous misjudgment. We had no longer any reason to continue farther up the Nile and, after taking on fuel, intended to turn the ship around and steam to Cairo. We would take up again the threads of our separate stories: an Alessandro Comi would return with Claudia to Benghazi to advocate the interests of our sponge industry (now that the plague was believed to have subsided); another would remain aboard *The Minos* and be beheaded by a pirate's scimitar while a third would paint in his Roman studio an extraordinary tableau: *A Swan Boat on the Nile.* "Look!" shouted the bear, which had a canvas chair folded under each burly arm. (Surely, he was a bear and not a man dressed up as one!) We turned our faces to the sun, rising or setting on the river's upper reach, and saw a royal barge on which a chorus and an orchestra (complete with ophicleide) performed *The Elijah Oratorio* of Mendelssohn's with an ardor to make the stolid ibis fly. Behind the barge the swan boat followed, with an Alessandro and Gordon Pasha—the former dressed in pajamas, the latter in a toga. They sat serenely in the shade of a floating blue canopy upheld at each corner by a cherub while the cataract men shouted, "*Yah Mohammed*!" On either shore, camels knelt and palms bowed before the slain hero and his rescuer. We lit cigars in their honor, and as the chorus was proclaiming Elijah's ascent in a flaming chariot, the swan boat began to rise (or so it seemed to us who were, admittedly, dazzled by the spectacle). "They are flying to Dyrehavsbakken to wake the sleeping women there," said Captain Seferiádhis, who had read it in *The Minos*'s log (unaware that we had forged an alternative future). Smiling, we laid wreathes of smoke on the ecstatic air; *and the words—on which we had been riding—stopped.*

THE TRANSFIGURATION OF ALESSANDRO COMI

His was a sadness too penetrating to be called by any other word than melancholy, in whose lexical remoteness he found an equivalent for the distance he felt—and sought to maintain—from the present. To pronounce it, which he did with the deliberateness of the connoisseur, reminded him of his solitude and also of his ridiculousness. He was unsuited to his age and knew it, but he could identify within himself few qualities that might have justified an agreeable feeling of superiority. He was like a man wearing a dinner jacket to a picnic: smugly confident of an inner correctness and, at the same time, self-conscious and embarrassed. He was hated by many, but he could summon no compensatory narcissism to allow him to suffer their ill will with equanimity. The truth was that he shared a little in their hatred. He had that predisposition to martyrdom the world finds unattractive.

I am writing in a manner that would have pleased him, however overwrought it strikes you, the reader of this ... elegy? Eulogy? Or is it in actuality a condemnation? Alessandro Comi was grotesque—not the man so much as the ideal to which he had pledged himself. In him survived a titanic energy, now all but spent, that had emulated nature's own decadence in the architecture of Camillo-Guarino Guarini, the paintings of Caravaggio, and the music of Pergolesi—all of whom Comi adored. He once read to me from Borges's preface to the 1954 edition of his first collection of stories, *A Universal History of Iniquity*: "I would venture to say that the Baroque is the final stage in all art, when art flaunts and squanders its resources." Borges might well have been commenting on the art of Alessandro Comi.

"It is untrue what they say about my writing," he had remarked. "It is not a triumph of mannerism over substance. The manner and the substance in my case are identical. I write not to express but to hide myself. My stories are like the chambered nautilus's shell: an exquisite and impregnable refuge." A man not given to confession, his candor had taken me by surprise. His conclusion had been equally disconcerting, though its logic was as inevitable as it was tragic. "Like the animal inside, I am trapped in my own production."

I saw Alessandro for the last time in Geneva, ten years after he had written that most Baroque of all his fictions, *A Swan Boat on the Nile*, which I had lately translated out of the Italian into English. I had done so not because I admired it (I admired it neither more nor less than a hundred other things), but because I wanted to give him a proof of my affection. During the war, he had hidden me until I could cross the mountains into Switzerland. Now I was in Geneva to give him the English book. He accepted it without a word, scarcely glancing at its cover as he put it into his coat pocket. I was annoyed; I had expected an effusion of gratitude. But his thoughts were elsewhere as were his eyes—fixed on the surface of the lake in which the sky had sunk so that, briefly, the lake seemed empty of water. My own eyes became rapt by the uncanniness of that scene in which a steamer, far out from shore, appeared to be making its slow way among islands of cloud. It was beautiful and strange, lasting only a few still moments while the wind held its breath. Soon enough, the wind revived and—the true sky having grown suddenly dark—the lake became itself again; and the boat was free to pursue its course unhindered by reflection. Alessandro rose and, taking my arm, walked with me to his room on the rue de Berne.

He boiled some coffee in silence, which we drank in silence. When we had done, he opened a clothbound ledger whose pages, I saw, were thatched with geometrical theorems and algebraic equations of a formidable complexity. They were meaningless to me, who am inept at mathematics.

"Yours?" I asked, and he answered with an affirmative nod. "I didn't know you understood such things."

He shrugged and smiled—a little vainly, I thought, although my judgment might have been colored by a natural envy of his extraordinary gifts.

"What does it mean?"

"I have been reading Hilton's novel *Lost Horizon*," he began. "When I was a young man, I pretended to despise it as intolerably romantic. But I confess that its romance, its longing for the remote, its desire to be beyond the furthest reaches of geography always have appealed to me. Lately, I have wanted—wanted is too weak a word to tell the strength of my desire—to climb the Mountains of the Blue Moon to Shangri-La."

I nearly laughed in his face, but something in his face stopped me.

"Norman, I have found a way," he said simply.

"A way to do what?" I was being obtuse, but he was talking about a fiction! There were no Mountains of the Blue Moon; Shangri-La was a schoolboy's dream. Hilton's novel was an act of the imagination at its most willful and indulgent. It was fantasy nearly erotic in its intensity—a "gaze" pornographic in its desire to possess what cannot be possessed.

I believed, then, in the obligation of literature to apply its powers of discourse to the solution of human problems. But my disapproval of his abdication of responsibility—a cowardice before reality—went unnoticed. He was intent on locating certain "*passages*" in the text; he used the English word deliberately for its double meaning, stressing it so that I would be sure to understand him.

"Hilton's text itself reveals the way in," he insisted.

"But into what?" I asked with an anger I did not then understand.

"Shangri-La," he said in a voice that made the word the very timbre of serenity.

"But that is only a story!" I nearly shouted.

"Yes," he said smiling. Then he read aloud the following passages, again stressing words he believed significant: "'But it was to the head of the valley that his eyes were led irresistibly, for there, soaring into the gap, and magnificent in the full shimmer of moonlight, appeared what he took to be the loveliest mountain on earth. It was an almost perfect *cone* of snow....'" And: "'Framed in the pale *triangle* ahead, the mountain showed again, gray at first, then silver, then pink as the earliest sunrays caught the summit.'" And: "'We've been slithering along the face of the *perpendicular* mountains for the last hour....'" And yet again: "'Beyond that, in a dazzling *pyramid*, soared the snow slopes of Karakal.' In each, Hilton has reduced features of an alien landscape to geometry."

He closed the book and—I swear!—kissed its cover

reverently as if that novel were a sacred text, which to him it was.

"There are numerous places where Hilton—consciously or not—indicated that the key to entering the lamasery at the top of the world is mathematics. Listen: 'Many were engaged in writing manuscript books of various kinds; one (Chang said) had made valuable researches into pure mathematics.' A literary text," Alessandro continued, "resembles a mathematical depiction in that they have only an apparent dimensional reality. In truth both exist in the mind where they refer to an actuality that can only be represented, never grasped. By exchanging one set of symbols for another, a story can be translated into the language of mathematics."

Tracing, as if the portal of a dream, one of the ideal forms inscribed in his ledger, he declared: "I have—how do I say it?—rendered Shangri-La into geometry and translated myself into such a mathematics as will allow me to enter it."

I thought him insane. So would you have, had you been there. I went to the window and watched a tram discharge its passengers in order to fasten onto something real. I might have been one of them, for it was to himself he continued speaking:

"To live beyond the reach of events, outside contingency, in an immutable—incorruptible—present that is nonetheless rich in intellectual and sensual pleasures— what would I not do? I might write my history, love, even found a dynasty in Shangri-La. I might have eternal life in Shangri-La in as much as Hilton made no provision for the death of his anonymous mathematician. And were I to perish in my interpolation, I have only to wait for a reader to resurrect me."

"You should try looking out the window!" I said, wanting to hurt him. "At those people getting off the tram. What is Shangri-La to them? Death is real and inescapable—even here, in neutral Switzerland."

Angered, I led the conversation along other paths. He followed reluctantly, his thoughts on the disturbing, but nonetheless entrancing, topology he had spirited onto his ledger's lined pages from his unusual imagination. After a while, having lapsed into silence, I left.

I did not think of Alessandro again (wanting to turn him out of my mind the way you would a troublesome boarder) until receiving, six or seven months after our meeting in Geneva, a package from him. In it was his copy of *Lost Horizon*. A corner of a page was turned down and in the margin written in Alessandro's hand was a complicated equation and, underlined in the peacock blue ink he always affected, the sentence: "... another [who had, by one way or another, found himself in Shangri-La] was coordinating Gibbon and Spengler into a vast thesis on the history of European civilization."

To write such a history had always been Alessandro's ambition. To imagine him vanished into the pages of a novel, however, is beyond any possibility I have power to entertain. While I never saw him again, the ordinary world has no shortage of hiding places.

The following month, I received a letter from the woman who had rented Alessandro his room on rue de Berne. She wrote that she had had crated his enormous collection of books and, if I were willing to accept them COD, she would send them to me in Philadelphia. Such, she continued, had been my friend's wish expressed in a letter left behind for her, together with—an unexpected largesse!—six months' rent.

I agreed at once.

Alessandro's library was as comprehensive as it was various. Not only did it include fictional works on fantastical and fabulous themes, but every important discipline of classical thought and art was represented.

Among the many volumes, I found none by Gibbon or Spengler.

I keep Alessandro's copy of *Lost Horizon* with me. (It is a small book and takes up little room.) I consider it a monument to my friend's obsession, or its grave.

I may know nothing about the higher forms of mathematics but am an adept in musical forms. While still a young man, I published a monograph on tempo in Handel's treatment of the *bourrée*, which was noticed kindly by the eminent Handel musicologist Rudolf Steglich. Perhaps it was that early leaning that attracts me to another of Hilton's passages, which Alessandro underlined, concerning the inhabitants of Shangri-La: "There were many tideless channels in which they dived in mere waywardness, retrieving, like Briac, fragments of old tunes." Who knows whether or not Briac might appreciate a protégé who shares his interest in ancient airs and dances? And what is there—I ask you—to keep me here?

PIECES
FOR SMALL
ORCHESTRA

We know that the history of the planets
is written in a circus tent.
—Faruk Ulay

For my Funambulist Wife, Helen

1.

The General is happy. He is playing hopscotch on the tiled floor with his own shadow. The tiles are black and white and perfect in the way of tiles. The shadows of his high boots stretch and break like Turkish taffy each time he reaches the apogee of his hopping, which is nothing laughable—no, not for one who was wounded long ago beneath the walls of Bór. The General is in love with the Hat-Check girl, as am I, who lacks the General's magnificent moustache and savoir faire. It is the insouciance that belongs to love alone that accounts for it—this hopscotching by the banquette "like a young man in the cavalry." The General has an assignation, later, in the Mediterranean Room when she has finished for the night. Until then, she promises to keep his sword safe among the hats. The General has given her a bag of sweets. She is young enough to be swayed by sweets, to be seduced by certain flavors. Their identity she keeps secret from him, else she will be at his mercy! All but invisible, she stands among the coats, smelling the night air on them. We are inside and happy to be so. Even the General, whose sword is merely ornamental now that he has been smitten by love. Possessed of an elastic heart, I go in search of the Cigarette-Girl. The palm leaves sway in the artificial breeze. The leisurely palm in its fat bronze pot. The orchestra, though small, has so far played from a repertory whose variety we have no right to expect in this second-rate hotel. The General's sword breathes in the dark of the coatroom, waiting for the heroic action to come. (The flavors are mango and melon.)

2.

The Prime Minister is in the vestibule, brushing his silk hat with his sleeve. He comes each night after the cares of state have been put away. He lays them in a drawer among maps and pairs of immaculate white gloves. To be here with us requires finesse, for the nation believes he is lucubrating, not waltzing—certainly not doing the two-step or tango with a rustling girl in his arms! A girl in a pale-yellow dress whose *frou frou* causes desire to rise up in his thinnest ducts. He left the ministry by the back stairs, eluded the stiffly standing military guard, and tiptoed past the alleys where, since nightfall, men and women have come in search of contraband. Each night he slides a stack of crimson inflationary currency over the sill of the wire wicket, behind which a woman sits who hands him in return a loop of blue tickets. Always it is the same girl with whom he dances—the one in the yellow dress, which makes a crepuscular music. She whose hair is the color of certain sunsets. It is for this the Prime Minister lives—not for his wife or countrymen, who pity him over their beer and sausages for his ceaseless devotion. I lift my glass to him as he passes near my table, but his mind is elsewhere—on a diagram of the samba he is now dancing, studied intently an hour ago (a map of movement through a space hostile to gracelessness). I know what is in his mind, for inside the hotel I have the gift of limited omniscience. Do not ask who gave me it. I don't know, unless it is the bottle of clearest gin, the mermaid on the swizzle stick, or the strength of my desire.

3.

The Engineer drinks too much. How else is he to discover a new planet—never mind the lineaments of a universe until now unrevealed to the mind of man? It is there, having swum nearly within his ken, just as it must have done for Ptolemy, Kepler, Tycho Brahe. "More chalk," he says to the Waiter, who brings him a stick from behind the bar. "Blue," he says; and the Waiter obliges with a dimpled cube from the billiard room. The Engineer, whose imagination was seized by the Palace of Running Water in Buenos Aires at an impressionable age, is on the threshold of discovery. We are glad for him. We, too, are interested in matters outside the ordinary, now that the ordinary is past enduring. "We are glad for you, Mr. Engineer!" we shout. He pretends not to be affected by our adulation as he bends over the table and composes the universe in blue chalk. We hope that it will be happier than the one we left outside the hotel, hostile and indifferent to art. Moved by a rare sympathy, the Prime Minister offers him one of his dance tickets so that he may enter a rhapsodic phase with a pretty girl in his arms; but he declines (with what regret we cannot say), choosing instead the selfless rigors of creation. I assure you, I would not have resisted—no, not for an instant, now that the entire orchestra is awake!

4.

Some want to hide. "Do whatever makes you happy!" we tell them (we, who are also, each in his own way, in hiding). There are closets and passages where one may conceal oneself; beds in the rooms upstairs, under which one may "lay low" for a while in perfect comfort. Some prefer to stand by the hour behind the heavy damask draperies. We take them beer and sandwiches and news of the orchestra: how the Bassoonist's sore throat is progressing, whether or not the Piccolo Player has found her embouchure. For all are interested in the condition of the orchestra. Without it the life of the hotel would cease and boredom—who knows?—drive us out onto the streets again (patrolled by armor-plated machines). And should we be bereft of essential services? We have provisioned ourselves with candles; boxes of government pamphlets wait to be burned; the storerooms are amply provided with tinned sardines, peaches, and baby peas. And the wine cellar seems in its apparently infinite recession into the darkness a sign of God's own largesse. Having renounced Clausewitz in favor of the caresses of our women, who prefer a polka to a Sousa march, the General has assessed the situation. "The situation," he assures us, "is brilliant. We have nothing to fear," he insists, pulling magisterially on his moustache. "We can survive a siege until we are relieved by those friendly to love." "And should they be delayed," we ask? The General shrugs and says, "For the better part of our lives then. And it is the better part that ought to concern us—the remnant suitable only for the grave." We are cheered, for we are still young and have not exhausted the pleasures of peace. I divest the Cigarette-Girl of her tray; together we ride the elevator to the roof, there to share a chocolate bar and exchange our astrological signs—mine, the Ram, hers, the Fish.

5.

"The anarchists have taken the moon." This news from the Journalist, who joined me at the bar for a gin and tonic. I was about to reply that they are welcome to it, for surely there are other moons: Io and Europa, for instance. But his crestfallen look silences me. "You are a romantic," I say, pleased to find tenderness in a war correspondent. He looks fondly at the colorful bottles ranged behind the bar. "Even Hemingway adored it," he says. "The Spanish moon, the Cuban. Ours is being held in a trolley barn at the end of the street. I don't think it minds," he says. "It must be tiresome," I reply, "to be always revolving." The Journalist opens his typewriter and begins to write his story, having assured me of his objectivity. I leave him to it and take the elevator to the rooftop lounge in order to confirm with my own eyes the truth: the sky is black where last night the moon shone full. What—I wonder— are their intentions toward it, the anarchists? Do they mean to ransom it, perhaps? But who is there now, among the enemies of poetry and celestial mechanics, who would pay to have the moon resume its rightful place? The times are bleak, the era inhumane, the age iron and dark. I return to the ballroom and watch a while the dancers compose intricate patterns on the parquet. I go into the Mediterranean Room and see, under a *trompe l'oeil* moon framed by an ornate trellis, the General and the Hat-Check girl embracing in the painted light.

6.

The Fireman is unhappy. They confiscated his engine and also his fire axe. "How am I to be a fireman without apparatus?" he asks. We have no answer. We give him a drink instead, so that he will know we are men and women of compassion. Our best single-malt Scotch, whose smoky taste we think will please him. It does; he drinks half the bottle. We withhold censure, knowing his desolation. We, too, have plumbed it, each after his own fashion. Each of us has tasted the bitter herbs. "Drink," we say, "and then sleep." We have a room prepared for him on the topmost floor so that he may look out upon the fires, which are raging here and there within the city. Having put him to bed, we confer among ourselves how best to solace him. "It would be well to have a fireman," says the Prime Minister. "One can no longer depend upon the city's infrastructure for essential services, now that civil war has ripped the social contract to shreds." "Firemen are colorful," says the Engineer, who is not (except for traces of blue chalk on his sleeves). "Not so colorful as generals!" asserts the General, who insists on precedence. He shows us his clocked socks. We go up and wait for the Fireman to wake. Inevitably he does. "This isn't the firehouse!" he cries, bewildered. "No, a hotel; and we wish to offer you the job of Fireman." We show him the apparatuses: the coiled hoses, the fire bottles, the shiny axes under glass. "But where is the pole?" he asks. We are embarrassed and shuffle our feet, not knowing what to say. He shakes his head dejectedly. "A fireman without a pole is a sad sort of fireman." "But we have other things," we tell him. "Cocktails and lobster bisque, chambermaids and a sauna. And imagine—our own movie theatre!" "Chambermaids?" he asks, clearly intrigued. "Yes, and Cuban cigars. There is also an orchestra which, though small and not always awake, plays with real fire." "With fire, you say?" "Figuratively so." "And the chambermaids are pretty?" "We have dreamed them to be beautiful and fluent in Romance languages. We have conceived everything to our complete satisfaction. All that we lacked was a fireman, an absence which we did not realize until now. Thank you, thank you for coming to our hotel!" "Am I, then, the only hotel fireman?" "You are solely it," we say, sensing victory. "And if I am too tired to wake in answer to the fire alarm?" "You may, if you like, battle the blaze in your sleep. The musicians sometimes play in theirs." "I would like," he says, "a cigar, a shave, and a red-haired chambermaid." "You have only to wish it for the secret ductwork of fulfillment to function sweetly." "I want happiness," he says, his eyes misting. "Happiness will be yours!" we promise. "In our hotel happiness is granted without reservation."

7.

"We don't need a stuffed rabbit," we tell him, "not even a galvanic one." The Taxidermist persists, though we turn our backs on him. "I have species that no longer exist on earth," he says. "We have a collection of mechanical animals, which amuses us," we answer him—anger flashing at the edge of our voices because of our wish to be dancing, now that the orchestra is playing with unusual brilliance. Later, at the bar after the orchestra has fallen asleep, we speak to him more civilly, cheered, perhaps, by the twinkling siphon bottles. "What we don't have is a river." The Hydrologist, mopping his perspiring face with a bar towel, asserts: "I am fabricating for you a river that will rival any in the real world, including the Amazon and the Nile." Indignant, the General quizzes him: "What do you mean by 'real'?" "That which is outside," the Hydrologist replies, "outside the hotel and which no longer concerns us." "Ah!" The instrumentalists wake; they were merely marshalling their orchestral forces. The General resumes the samba, which he performs with aplomb to the accompaniment of his spurs. He was in the cavalry! "What about fish?" asks the Taxidermist as we are once more drawn to the dance floor. "I have some remarkable examples from an earlier century, in attitudes that will remind you of harem girls. They are—I assure you—waterproof; and with this cunning motor, I can make them move!" He takes from his pocket a stuffed mouse and, unscrewing its head, shows us a tiny device. The Hydrologist is delighted. "An improvement over your windup model," he informs the Engineer with a disdain that makes me want to beat the brute. "I agree," says the Building Inspector, who has within his jurisdiction all things mechanical, including fish. The General despises technology, preferring his antique sword to a howitzer. "Windup fish are absolutely charming!" he says, kissing the Hat-Check on the nape of her neck. "Charming!" she giggles. "O, go to bed!" the Prime Minister screams; and they do—at once. "Welcome," the P.M. says, "to our hotel!" The Taxidermist bows. "I look forward to seeing the happy results of your collaboration with the Hydrologist." The Hydrologist offers the Taxidermist his arm, and they begin to dance the polka.

8.

The Building Inspector reports that the hotel's foundation is unsound. "Unsound!" we scoff. "Illusory," he declares, smacking his lips. "In fact, it can be said to exist in imagination only—in the wish that it *be*. There are no load-bearing walls, only cleverly painted screens that shift from day to day. I suspect the building is supported by the orchestra alone, by its playing or in its sleep—who knows?" "I dream of foundations," the General says, stroking his iron moustache; "foundation *garments*!" "Old *roué*!" we laugh, having long ago accepted his lasciviousness, inevitable in a general of cavalry as is his swagger stick. In his youth, he luxuriated on damascene pillows in the Kasbah. "We love you, General!" we cry, momentarily overcome by *bonhomie*. Beaming, he goes off in search of the Hat-Check, whom he adores. We resume our discussion of the foundation. "Only this morning I went to the cellar for a bottle of Gordon's Gin," I tell them. "While I did not—I admit— touch them, the walls looked to me substantial." The Hydrologist and the Taxidermist, who are inseparable, speak as one: "We can attest to bedrock. The progress of our river construction has been slowed because of it." The Archaeologist concurs, "I have discovered the fossilized record of an ancient settlement on the riverbed. I am writing a monograph, which I have no doubt will assure my fame." The Building Inspector, who is after all a realist, snickers: "You are, all of you, living in a dream world!" We do not dispute this. But whose? "You share a common delusion. But you must know that even a building that does not exist can collapse if it ignores the principles of construction." "Or catch fire," the Fireman remarks, "if not built strictly to code." "I suggest I make a thorough study and report back to you next year," the Building Inspector concludes. "Or the year after," we say with a magnanimous gesture of our seigniorial hand (the one we keep for occasions such as this, for ours is a world of pomp and circumstance). Upstairs, the General and the Hat-Check embrace on the ceiling. Applauding, we commission the hotel Photographer to record the moment with all his art, for love soon spends itself no matter how we will it otherwise.

9.

"How is it the hotel is without an astronomer?" we say one to another beneath the ballroom ceiling, whose elaborate chandeliers remind us of Lamaître's, which are said to be rushing with us through the universe. "Surely if we are to be a dying civilization's ark, we must have an Astronomer to enchant us with the radiant beauties on our way, such as the Pleiades, who count among their forebears Night and the titans who rule the outer seas!" Our hopes for the Engineer, whose planetary obsessions were nurtured assiduously by the hotel Barman, have come to naught because of his addiction to gin slings and Victor Herbert operettas. He sleeps now, his cheek resting on the wet rings imprinted by his glass—his head filled with cosmic dust and dreams of Naples and naughty Marietta. "My God!" we cry, beating the air with our fists. "We are hurtling into a japanned jar!" Aroused by our lamentation, the orchestra plays a nocturne whose principal theme is the heart in winter. It stirs in me yearning for summery loves—pitiable in the ice-cold pockets of space. I call for an anchovy sandwich (love and anchovies joined in my mind by an obscure equation of desire). "This is not the time!" the Prime Minister in his striped trousers rebukes me. "This is not the time for small fish!" Sullenly I fold a railroad timetable into a diminutive steam-locomotive. "Charming!" the General declares. "A perfect evocation of the Steam Age in which I reached maturity." A sudden ragged blush betrays an amorous memory. The orchestra troops noisily into the casino to play baccarat. The Prime Minister admonishes us, thus: "If we are not careful of digression, we'll lose ourselves among the unpredictable trajectories of a French curve!" "I adore French curves!" says the General slyly, so that even the Prime Minister laughs. The dumbwaiter door creaks open, and an Astronomer is delivered into our midst! We know him at once by his telescope. "I have been visiting the moon," he tells us. "I measured its luminosity and fed it sugar-cubes. It sits in the trolley barn with its light turned low and moos. I do not think it is happy." We beg him to stay with us and be the hotel's Astronomer. He agrees but must—he says—rest a while before taking up his duties, however light. The Chambermaid makes up a bed. He lies down and recites the history of his losses, which are also somehow ours: a comet seen one evening when he was young, a planet known only to him but by him now forgotten, stars swum off long ago beyond the telescopes of nostalgia, a girl whose eyes he serenaded beneath the balcony of the moon as it roamed the mansions of the sky.

10.

Enamored yet of night, the Astronomer no longer cares for the sky and its shining stenographs, preferring the hotel's fifth cellar kept dark at the request of the Agronomist. "There are edible roots to be considered," he says, "such as the turnip and potato, whose eyes like those of children with measles must not be exposed to light." But his opinions are radical, and we send him to count aphids on the potted palms. "Let us banish the Astronomer to the streets!" the Prime Minister fulminates. "The

General tickles my ear with his cavalry moustache as he whispers the story of the P.M.'s latest folly—this, with the Chambermaid, who spurned him. To be made an object of derision by young women infuriates the P.M. always, but he is helpless against their enchantments. We give him money for the Soubrette, who will allay his injury with comic songs. "The Astronomer ought, at least, to be impeached," the Maître d' affirms after the elevator door has closed on the Prime Minister's swallow-tailed coat. "We gave him sanctuary so that he might score the grand recessionals of space. Instead, he spends his time with the Hydrologist, underground." "Good God!" says the General, putting his hand on his hilt. "You don't suppose they are in love?" I answer that the Hydrologist is faithful to his obsession. "Which is?" "To discover an underground lake like that beneath the Paris Opera House, where the Phantom rowed his boat." The General draws his sword and reminisces, "I saw Christine Daë the night of her triumphant debut. I was a young lieutenant of horse at the time. Gad! I was smitten!" In homage to his youth, he cuts a sash cord with a single swash. The window falls, a dirty pane shivers into light. "Look there!" the General exclaims, pointing outside to a wheel of phosphor. "A new galaxy! I shall name it after me as is my right." He preens myopically in the lobby mirror. "I'll be Astronomer and General, both!" He asks for my admiration, and I give it to him gladly although his galaxy is a clock atop a warehouse roof—half its numbers cold as space itself through which we, inside our hotel of illusion, drift. "We must drink to it," he says. And do.

11.

The Engineer dismantles the anemometer, which pumped by means of belts a bellows-organ through our nights. Weather and its influence have been abolished. To be exact, our interest in it—once paramount—is no more. The organ, however, will be missed, now that the orchestra's recalcitrance has made a hash of our musical evenings. We must have music if for no other reason than to fence in time, which last week was dismissed as superfluous. Anarchy succeeds tyranny always, and we who fled the thralldom of the Absolute approve the succession with our minds, though our hearts may yearn for clocks and snow and the ironed precision of a military band. Having bivouacked on the Russian Steppes, the General does not protest against weather's banishment. The Meteorologist, however, is aggrieved: "You've made of my life a Zero!" His unseemly shout causes the orchestra leader to raise his baton. "Weather is for me," the Meteorologist asserts, "a passion, a vocation, an infatuation. I will hang myself at once if it is not restored." To forestall this act of self-slaughter, the Analyst entrances him with his dazzling *pince-nez*. Euphoric after an afternoon of fox-trots, the Prime Minister inclines toward mercy. "He may woo his weather *inside* the hotel," he says, tugging at a French cuff. "How so?" I ask. "We shall allow him to introduce inclemency into our equable atmosphere. A tropical depression, a sudden fall of millibars, a *soupçon* of instability will be tonic and may—who knows?—wake the orchestra." We cheer his good sense and elect him by acclamation to another term. All but the General, who is dreaming of vodka and the Russian Saber Dance. The Fireman lights an Abdullah; tricked by its smoky blue arabesques, the sprinklers in the ballroom ceiling rain. "O, this is more like it!" exclaims the Meteorologist, dripping wet. "I shall get my pluviometer and issue bulletins on the hour!" Ecstatic, he skips away to his weather station—all thought of grievance put away in his heart's drawer. The Hat-Check moves about the ballroom distributing black umbrellas. There stirs in every one of us a moist sensation akin to love for the old earth and the life—no longer possible for us—outside the hotel. Under his ministerial brolly, the P.M. exults: "The orchestra is awake!" The musicians have indeed taken up their instruments and stagger in the rain into a funeral march. Our eyes shed rain of their own, but we are not downcast, knowing that the weather of the heart is variable and absurd.

12.

Moustache stiff with macaroon, the fickle General spirits the Chanteuse down the cellar stairs, as if delivering her from the gallows. He is no more in step than Clauswitz with modern military science, yet it pleases her how his sword rattles on the floor when he dances the mazurka. His breath is pepperminted, his boots shine, his epaulets quake in expectation of her kisses, which have been mainly chaste. He has promised her, if not the moon, a lunar simulacrum until he can work out to the last detail a brilliant strategy for lifting the siege laid to the actual moon (with a *divertissement* supplied by the musicians if they will only waken). "Where the Astronomer is," he declares, "there must inevitably be astronomy!" He draws her dreaming after him down flights of ringing metal steps into the fifth basement where the black lake is. He longs to take her in still puissant arms and press with strength of ardor her lissome body raptly to his decorated heart. (For displays of parade-ground equitation, valor against the Hun, for protocol on clay court and lawn, for shuttlecock diplomacy and the severity of his trousers' creases.) "But where," the General wonders, "is the Astronomer?" "Gone," answers the Engineer, who is winding a clockwork swan. "Where gone?" "Beneath the black lake." "How gone?" "In a submarine belonging to Jules Verne," replies the Engineer, nesting the swan among a wedge of its mechanized kind. The feathers are real—a gift of the Taxidermist, whose heart and blood are warm. "What is this place?" the General asks. "A pleasure park, a tryst and rendezvous for lovers. You are the first." The General blushes, but in the darkness who is there to see it? "Look!" exclaims the Chanteuse. "Stars!" Stars, indeed, are trembling on the surface of the lake (or so it seems). The General is delighted: "I expected a moon—tin painted with radium, hung from a wire. Such a thing as that would have been enough to make my Chanteuse sing. But stars—how can stars be where there is no sky?" "Reflections of the glittering mica and the shining schist," explains the Geologist, who with a little hammer was hiding in a seam of rock. "Geology is also beautiful, though my eyes are focused mostly on the ground." A Gondolier sings a barcarole in the dark, and the Chanteuse swoons into the General's arms— overcome by emotion, the engine by which all things move inside our hotel. Song at an end, the gondola drifts among *arpeggios* of silence, disturbing a mineral galaxy, which might have entranced Orpheus during his infernal hunt for Eurydice.

13.

To please the Funambulist (who one afternoon arrived—to our surprise—at an upstairs window by telegraph line), we string tightropes beneath each ceiling. Now she need not ever leave the air where she is in her element. I suffer to have her out of reach and twice try to step out on the high-wire to fondle her muscular calves—dangerous without a net. She is an artist descended from the *saltimbanques* Picasso painted rose. "I don't approve of her traipsing overhead!" the Prime Minister complains. "She gives me a crick in the neck!" The P.M. is alone in his irritation. The General and I stare raptly, when she passes, at her furbelows. "I would like," he says, "to make love in midair, balanced on the wire by my cavalry moustache. But alas, I am a victim of aerophobia, though I have dallied on a horse and once, in Bangalore, on an elephant with a maharaja's daughter. I hid my face in her frangipanied hair and wept for happiness!" Aroused, the General goes in search of the Chanteuse to show her scars a sepoy made during the famous Mutiny. The Astronomer, were he only here, would gaze in fascination at the airborne beauty's transit. But he is in a submarine on his way to Paris. "The Funambulist believes herself to be self-sufficient and aloof," the Telepath remarks, "when it is my paranormal mind, which keeps her poised." I beg him to let her fall into my arms. "She is—I swear it!—the sole object of my passionate regard." O, the inconstancy of some men's love! "I would kiss her slippered feet if once they came within proximity of my lips!" But the Telepath, who can bend spoons with his eyes, is afraid. "It may be," he says, "that it is she, after all, who dreams us while she walks upon the wire—a somnambulist in a dark and empty hotel. You do not know how the mind, like a Magic Lantern, projects images of desire onto the world." I shake him by his shoulders, shouting: "So long as I am in her arms, or seem to be!" I am not so attached to life to regret if it should prove illusory. The orchestra wakes and plays "*Valse Triste.*" The Telepath cannot master his tears, nor can I my desperate yearning. Lightly the Funambulist lifts up on to her toes—in despite of telepathy, gravity, and sorrow—as if to forsake her attachment to the earth. The Engineer brings me a tall stepladder (the one used to dust the chandeliers), and I climb and cling to her sweet knees just in time to kiss them one by one.

14.

"Who let in the elephants?" shouts the Engineer, afraid for the beams beneath the ballroom floor, which were never meant for pachyderms. We admire his devotion to our welfare and propose a loving-cup be given him, inscribed with an S and an N—the alchemical symbol for tin. The idlers loafing in the loggia cheer in affirmation. The Prime Minister, however, speaks gravely concerning the absence of ordinances governing elephants and assembles his cabinet to enact them. The elephants have gravitated to the potted palms, stirring remembrance in their small brains of Ceylon—for these elephants are Indian. The General recalls his youthful amours, when a subaltern on the Subcontinent, inside a *howdah.* "*Howdah*?" We are bemused by this unusual word, whose part of speech we cannot even guess at. "A noun," the General says definitively, so that there can be no doubt. He draws for us a *howdah,* on a cocktail napkin with the little yellow pencil favored by gin-rummy addicts for keeping score. It looks—the *howdah* does—like a house perched on an elephant's back. Above its roof of thatch or silken damask is a moon thin, curved, and coppery as a scimitar's blade. The hotel Carpenter sets to work at once, for we are all enchanted by the *howdah*'s erotic possibilities. The elephants, meanwhile, are shaking with their trunks the tightrope where my Funambulist is pursuing her extraterrestrial vocation. She tries to shoo them with her parasol, but they only laugh, or seem to, in Esperanto. "Look!" the Photographer cries, eyes blinded by the magnesium flash with which he captured an elephant in the corner. It must be shy. "Look, the orchestra is awake!" It is, indeed, and playing what in circus slang is called a screamer. "But there is none!" I tell the musicians, much annoyed. "There is no circus here, only elephants!" Crestfallen, the musicians clink and rattle and bang *en masse* into the Desert of Sinai Room to swell the klezmer band. "There ought to be!" the Cigarette-Girl says, her smoky voice creped in disappointment. "There ought to be a circus for us to go to when we're blue!" A tear slides out one eye like a raindrop down a windowpane. I take her in my arms and vow to lobby for a circus. Unmoved by pretty girls who cry, the Zoologist is adamant that what is needed is a zoo! The Cigarette-Girl slaps him. He slaps her back, in reprisal. "Why not both?" the Fireman intervenes, brandishing an ax to persuade the combatants to reconcile. "There are enough of the mammoth mammals for a zoo and circus, too." I telegraph an invitation to the Funambulist to be—above the circus's center-ring—the cynosure. Disdainfully she semaphores her answer: I PREFER TO PRACTICE MY ART UNDISTRACTED BY

THE PEANUT-MUNCHING CROWD, CANNON-CATAPULTED MEN & BEASTS HOWEVER GAY. The Musicologist protests that Stravinsky composed *Circus Polka* for fifty Barnum & Bailey elephants, with dance-steps by Balanchine. "Art and circuses," he reminds us, "are not antithetical." But she is unswayed on her high-wire by his argument—a woman altogether remote from us and our petty dreams inside the hotel.

15.

"The reason for your shame lies, as always, inside the unconscious mind," the hotel's Analyst pronounces. I am on his couch, spellbound by swirling blue cigar smoke. He apes his idol, Freud; in fact, begs to be called Sigmund, though his name is Frank. "Don't you adore," he says, "the Talking Cure, the hours hunting in the mire of your repressions for the cause of all this hurt?" "I should like a tranquilizer," I answer, "or an outlawed drug." "Did you dream last night?" he asks, leaning toward me with his hand cupped to an ear so as not to miss the slightest intimation of a harrowing that will explain my disquiet. I am enthralled by a shred of tobacco leaf clinging to his lower lip. He mistakes my interest for evidence of libido. I begin to speak and am teleported on the couch (without sensation of transit) to the Theatre of Cruelty Room. "How was it done?" "By a psychic Super-Conductor," he smirks. I am too inert to hate him, but will when he has cured me of my lethargy. The orchestra is awake and playing a *danse macabre* in a corner of the room, whose principal decorations are peacock feathers (emblematic of death for Victorians, who nonetheless kept them in their parlors). "It is for their 'eyes' that I admire them," the

Analyst remarks, climbing onto the couch with me. He closes his and sleeps. Under the argus of feathers trembling in the draft, I reenact my dreams—beginning with one in which I am in the ballroom, dancing in my underpants. The orchestra changes its tune. "It is a common dream," the Bassoonist says, waiting for his entrance at the 32nd bar. "I dream it often." I continue with my oneiric recollection: Charlotte Corday has dispatched Marat in his bath and turns, holding still the gory knife. With mayhem clearly on her mind, she staggers to me while the musicians play a rumba. "In the name of the Revolution, I will chop you!" says the homicidal mademoiselle. Not till now have I noticed how much like an abattoir the room is. "You are a fantasist deserving death!" she denounces in the voice of the Analyst, which makes me wonder if he has not thrown it into one of the Engineer's automatons. "This is the reason for your shame." I scream as the orchestra climaxes. "How do you feel?" the Analyst asks, rising from the couch. Charlotte and the bloody tub are gone. Were they figures in my dream, or his? The eyes gaze at me with disdain. The musicians put down their instruments. The Analyst dictates into an antique Ediphone. I rush from the room while "death wish" issues from his bloodless lips.

16.

I hurry down the metal stairs to the hotel's deepest cellar (deeper than the river the Hydrologist is dreaming into being) where the Engineer has built a trysting place for love. Breathless, I lean against the newel. Brume gone from my eyes, I look into the darkness, which lies like soot (not soot—like black pearls pestled into powder), and see

70

no sign of couples seized by love. It is for them I hurried underground. But the spot conceived as a pleasure park is empty except for me and swans no longer pink in this tenebrous light that does not shine so much as pierce the body like a draft of hell. I hear groaning such as a great iron door might make on obdurate hinges (or Dante's damned) and turn to see a gondola heaving into view. I am glad of this much life as I wait for the Gondolier. But the boatman who greets me is not Venetian but one who ferries the dead while his boat's grim pennants snap in the still and fetid air. It is Charon in his black boat (not a gilded gondola at all!), who rows toward me with a face of stone. It is the oars in their locks that groan. "You have sought death," he says, "and death has come to meet you, amiably." "I haven't!" I shout. But each word turns to glass as if produced by the mouth of a glassblower's pipe; and in each transparent sphere, I see myself embracing Death, whose womanly arms are white and slender. The Analyst throws his voice from where he is dreaming my neurosis on his couch: "You are in love with Death, and I have conjured Charon from your subconscious depths." The Analyst is mad! "Life," he says, "is not the *commedia del-arte*!" Mad, I tell you! "Death is the only therapy— that, or you must go out onto the streets again." That hell! The boat's prow sings a threnody among the reeds against the shore. The boatman shows me instruments of self-slaughter: noose, knife, loaded gun, and a noisome vial that will—he tells me with his mind—bring surcease from pain. I choose the poison. But before I can drink it, the orchestra wakes and plays a waltz so leadenly I might have drowned if the lovely Funambulist, who vowed never to leave her high-wire, had not come down and rescued me.

17.

Tomorrow, I shall wed the Funambulist, who has resumed her lonely orbiting above our heads—aloof from desire, rancor, and the vagaries of the musicians, whose music is to her as a rustling of dry leaves, concert programs, and trolley transfers soft and pastel as lingerie (which she neglects sometimes to wear—to the General's infinite delight, and mine). "Will you," I asked her yesterday from a step-ladder's topmost rung while she pedaled a unicycle used by those of her aerial profession, "marry me?" She wobbled uncertainly (the General and Prime Minister gasped!) before regulating her course with the balancing-pole she never goes without. "I"—she began and finished an hour later when her circular peregrination brought her back again—"will." "How is it to be managed?" the General asks as the Barman performs an act of effervescence with a siphon bottle. "What?" I inquire with my eyes, which are crossing sottishly. We are drinking Scotch and soda. "Cheers!" the General says, quaffs, wipes his gray moustache, snuffles, finishes at last his question: "Love on a high-wire? I would not risk it now that I am old, but in my youth, I would have!" The Funambulist, whom I adore, has sworn never to leave again the air for common ground. "I have not considered it," I admit. "Not?" "No." "Why not?" "It slipped my mind." The General is aghast. "Well, you must—it is essential— the *raison d'être* and *sin qua non* of love!" "I shall love her mentally," I tell him. "*Pah!*" The General is disgusted. "Then I will learn to walk the wire like her," I say, "and make love in midair as swifts and hawks do." Indifferent to ornithology, the General observes that bliss is achieved easiest in bed with champagne, dim lights, and a record crooning on the gramophone. "Life," he declares, "is theater and must, like it, have furniture, properties, and music!" "But she will not come down!" I cry, startling the hotel guests arriving with swizzle-sticks, silver fish-forks, and other wedding gifts. The Engineer (master of expediency) presents me, shyly, his: a kind of wristwatch which, when worn, will help me rise to the occasion. It contains a tiny gyro and device designed by Count Ferdinand von Zeppelin. "With it"—the Engineer colors crimson—"you will achieve the necessary lightness." I am overcome and cannot find words to tell him thanks. In their turn the General promises a jeroboam of Taittinger from Reims, the Photographer aerial photos in *chiaroscuro*, the Electrician romantic lighting of varied hue and lumen. "Now all that remains is a musical accompaniment to our union!" I exclaim. The orchestra cannot be counted on—this, we have learned during our days and nights in the hotel. In answer the endlessly revolving Funambulist whisks past on her cycle, and we hear how the wind in her hair plays a serenade for strings. "Thank you for this dream!" I call to her, throwing kisses. "Tonight, I will levitate with miniature moons left by the Astronomer in his trunk and adorn your fingers, your ears, and the tips of your breasts. And after tomorrow, I will spend my nights suspended from your lips like a trapeze artist—in despite of gravity and death."

18.

Distraught, the Journalist has withdrawn to his room— to the bathtub in it where he lies uncomfortably on the porcelain bottom to mortify himself with the aid of Irish whiskey and cigarettes. The Prime Minister, hanged by ruffians during a *coup d'etat*, explains that the Journalist mourns his lost life of action. (The P.M. perished, nearly, because of the rope's shoddiness.) "He is one," the Prime Minister says, "whose career has been lit by conflagration, the meteoric rise and fall of men, and the magnesium flash with which his photographer captured scenes of mayhem." (Not the hotel's Photographer, whose work appeared in glamour magazines, but another who kept his film in bandoliers and died.) The General enters with the Chanteuse on his arm, and we encourage her to coax the Journalist from the tub. "I'll sing a song to make him forget the world outside, which is not ours: an *aubade* made famous by Finnish vocalist Laila Kinnunen." Listening, we are moved to tears, which rain into the bath—all but the Journalist, who does not shed any. "I am surfeited," he confesses, "by the sybaritic pleasures of this hotel." "Even love?" scoffs the General. A romantic in *fin de siècle* Paris, he kissed a girl in Fingal's Cave to hear her heart resound. "Would you care for a can-can dancer?" asks the hotel Choreographer, pockets stuffed with peanut brittle. But the Journalist looks away—pained! "I must," he says, "go into the streets again and practice my profession, which is to record events no matter how unpleasant. I must be an amanuensis to the age in which we find—by chance—ourselves." The Financier turns from his image in the bathroom mirror, where he has been trimming his Vandyke, and offers to fund a newspaper complete with Linotype and presses made in Heidelberg. But the Journalist is determined. "Then interview the moon!" enjoins the General, never having entirely renounced the habit of command. "We wish to know its condition and if the anarchists will release it from imprisonment inside the trolley barn—and" (unfolding a map created by the Chamber of Commerce) "news of other casualties of civil war such as" (pointing with a finger at them) "the Botanical Garden, spumoni factory, and The Café of the Troubadours." The Journalist rises from his bath (Marat did not) and, with his portable Underwood, goes (after having dressed!) out the door. "I think we shall not see him again," the P.M. remarks matter-of-factly, for he was trained as a diplomat to dissemble. Only the Chanteuse is affected. "He was, for all his inner torment, sweet." In her red-rimmed eyes, I see her horror of us all. The orchestra plays a melancholy air suitable for departures as we go down to lunch.

19.

It is, as the Hydrologist suspected, true: the black lake beneath the hotel communicates by underwater passages with that below the Paris Opera where Christine Daë— abducted for love!—was made to gaze upon the Phantom's face. The boat he rowed through granite vaults, singing *lieder* (his voice no more pleasing than the rest of him), arrives one day with the Phantom on it. He is shy, afraid we will shun him for his beastly conduct. But we have forgiven him long ago his errors. We, too, know the madness of unrequited love. "You are welcome to our hotel," the General says, pressing upon him gifts from his uniform's pockets: a cigar from Havana, blue tickets entitling him to dance with any girl he fancies, a banana, and a fountain pen "for autographs." The Phantom is sure to be a popular addition to hotel life! "You are welcome to stay as long as you like." It is understood, however, that the mask must remain *in situ* on the Phantom's face, for we have expelled ugliness from our world, which is not the real one. The Phantom bows, and does a thing with his cape that is best described as courtly. We lead him upstairs to a reception room copied from the Paris Opera House's to put him at his ease. "How kind!" he mumbles through his mask. "How very good you are to me!" In recognition of his rehabilitated reputation, the orchestra plays one of his own compositions. "You play with *élan*," he says. "I have seldom heard it so!" Now the Prime Minister makes a speech in which he praises love, music, and détente. We are moved and stand in line to kiss the Phantom on the cheek as though he were a jilted groom. The analogy is not lost on him; he cries onto his sleeve because he has no bride. Now it is the Phantom's turn to stand upon the dais and address us: "My friends, I [...]." We did not hear him end, because of his mask and the microphone, which dropped. His hand was numb with rowing! We give him an ovation so as not to shame him for his *contretemps*—a man who has suffered humiliation for an accident of birth, or acid. The gong is rung; we sit at table according to protocol and precedence: the Prime Minister at one head, the General at the other. The Phantom is seated between two women to prove we feel not the slightest repugnance. The mask remains in place—cumbersome prosthesis that would have precluded eating if the Chef had not thought to serve linguini. The evening is a success! Every course is greeted with applause. The Phantom raves about the pâté de foie gras, begging for the recipe—a request that ordinarily would offend the Chef, the points of whose moustache are catching fire now because of his culinary *éclat*. Or so it seems to me, whose happiness is completed by the timely passing of my bride, the Funambulist, overhead. "Thank you for giving me sanctuary in your story— mine was finished!" the Phantom cries before collapsing, exhausted by his awful rowing all the way from France. The Taxidermist, who has been kneading wax, rushes to his side. Once an apprentice of Madame Tussaud's, he hopes to replicate the Phantom for an exhibition of hotel curiosities. But we will not permit this outrage to a sleeping guest! The Photographer is allowed one picture for the hotel magazine. "Carry him to bed!" the General orders; and we do. He weighs nothing as you might have guessed a phantom would. He looks so small in the bed the Chambermaid has made for him that pity for this traduced character of melodrama grips us. I turn out the lights. The Chanteuse sings a lullaby. We tiptoe from the room, our hearts enlarged by fellow feeling. Why can't real life be like this? A bomb goes off outside, rattling the ballroom chandelier in answer.

20.

Not even the orchestra at its most *fortissimo* can muffle the denotations, which from time to time remind us of life outside the hotel. When it happens that an anarchist's bomb goes off somewhere near, anxiety seizes us even in the middle of a foxtrot. Fear besets us, and the Building Inspector and the Analyst are sought—one to assess the effect of this latest strain on the building's load-bearing walls, the other to measure how trauma may have injured our minds' soft tissues. "What is common to our inquiries," they say in unison, "is the vulnerability of this fragile enterprise to stress." We shudder, knowing now the world cannot entirely be shut out—not even by our dreamers, who sleep in round-the-clock shifts, and poets, who scarcely stop to think. Suicide is much discussed, should we be overrun by reality. Escape routes are mapped to the cellar where the lake is. The gondolas and swan boats on it are stocked with liquor and chocolate, their windup motors oiled. "We are not always at risk," our resident Physicist explains. "The hotel is a vibration of our common desire: a periodic movement of particles in suspension." His thinking is shaped by String Theory, which we adore, though do not understand. "The hotel leans into and out of harm," he explains with laudable patience for our layman's resistance, "like a lovely girl on a swing painted in oil by Fragonard. A girl with pink and rosy skin, who may be nude! She moves into the afternoon light and returns to the arboreal shade. Just so are we by lazy alternation visible to the world and then invisible, in all twenty-six dimensions. Back and forth, back and forth," he intones like a pendulum, putting the orchestra to sleep—all but the Strings, who are interested in his theory. "If only we could stop time in its tracks," the Chanteuse says, "while we are in the invisible segment of the arc inscribed from garden to trees!" "Theoretically we might ride a Von Stockum Band to an earlier time," the Physicist muses. "To the Napoleonic Wars!" exclaims the General. "To Charcot at Salpêtrière to study hysteria in women!" cries the Analyst. "To Fulton's steamboat!" effuses the Engineer, who as a boy had a miniature one. "To the mammoths and mastodons of the Pleistocene!" the Taxidermist snarls in a manner altogether sanguinary and obscene. The Physicist retires to his mind to give the matter further thought. Another explosion rattles the windows in their sashes; a plaster cupid tumbles from a cornice in the ballroom built in praise of lust. "This cupid's real," the Engineer states categorically. "It is and isn't," replies the Philosopher smugly. "It is a real plaster-of-Paris cupid!" the Engineer declares, shaking his fist in a fury of frustration. This fact the Philosopher acknowledges: "I grant you that." "The hotel is not invisible!" the Engineer shouts, loudly enough for the Physicist to hear. "It is and isn't," the Philosopher returns to his theme. We hurry to our seats to listen to them wrangle, willingly suspending our disbelief. "By the strength of the imagination can buildings rise (Gaudí's Casa Battló, for example). And by it are they made both visible and invisible." "It is the same with love," I say softly, looking up as my Funambulist bride crosses on her high-wire—seen for a moment, then not.

21.

The Hydrologist has not been seen for a time that seems inordinate, though it may be otherwise here where duration, like a rubber band, is uncertain. We send him telegrams sung by the Chanteuse in a *coloratura* that charms carp from the depths of the canal he has been digging with an industry blind to necessity and sleep—a virtual Suez without an ounce of concrete in it. Nor is the desert sand a mineral composition but, rather, a musical one. The Hydrologist, whose specialty is channels of liquid distribution, was entranced by the musicians' playing a Sigmund Romberg operetta in their sleep. "He scarcely looked at me," says the Chanteuse, unbuttoning her Western Union blouse while in bed the General waits with tremulous emotion. "I am sorry for him." "Feel sorry for me!" he cries like a child general. "You are making me wild as a bull elephant!" The Telepath has turned us into voyeurs sitting in a ring, hands clasped in one another's, to witness this bedroom farce. Ennui is demoralizing in men as weak as we, whose indecent gaze might have persisted had the Hydrologist not shouted from offstage: "Eureka!" He can be forgiven his unoriginality; he is dry as dust in every aspect of his life save water. We find him on the cellar stairs, leading by a filthy bandage an Egyptian mummy. "By accident, I cracked open the lid of its sarcophagus with a pickaxe!" Our liquid specialist is close to tears, overwrought with ambivalent emotion. "I didn't mean to disturb its eternal rest," he says; "but, ladies and gentlemen, what a thing to find!" We flinch because of the odor. "It stinks!" exclaims the Plumber, an expert in the unsavory arts. "Remove it!" Indignant, the Hydrologist refuses: "It will reveal to us the secrets of the pyramids and the meaning of the Sphinx." "Does it speak?" asks the Prime Minister—himself until this moment speechless. But the Hydrologist has yet to pose a question to his shabby protégé. "How many constellations did Amenhope's *Catalogue of the Universe* contain?" the Chambermaid, graduate of the Sorbonne, inquires to satisfy our common curiosity. "Did Cleopatra look like Claudette Colbert?" the Manicurist quizzes it. She is a film historian when she is not filing nails. The Mummy does not respond to either interlocutor. Is it mute, willful, or are its brains buried by the Nile in a canopic jar? "I shall read its mind," says the Telepath. "Yes, do!" the Analyst urges. "I should like to map its mental landscape—its compulsions, torments, and desires." The Telepath takes the Mummy's hand, shudders (as do we in sympathy!), shuts his eyes, concentrates with strength enough to bend a spoon. "What do you see?" the Analyst asks.

"Birds mostly with, here and there, a snake." "Ah! It dreams of flight or wriggling its way from the tomb," the Analyst avers with intolerable conceit. "No doubt it is a dream life rich in latent content. I should like to try my thought-extractor on it," he says, shoving the unraveling mummy toward his couch. "No!" the Hydrologist shouts; "it's mine!" The Prime Minister, whose diplomatic skills have been sharpened by disputes regarding the hotel's women, proposes to cut the mummy in half. Bored by their wrangling, the musicians play Sigmund Romberg's "Desert Song." The mummy dances as if afflicted by a disorder of its nervous system! "Interesting, though unorthodox," the hotel's Choreographer admits. "It might be possessed by Hathor, goddess of love, dance, and alcohol." "What's happening?" The General enters the lobby, looking pleased as would anyone having recently experienced love's quavers and demi-quavers. "Is that an Egyptian?" "A mummified one," replies the P.M. "Ah! In Cairo I knew several while a subaltern attached to Lord Kitchener's staff. Decent fellows, if a bit stiff. I'm dying for a gin!" We adjourn to the barroom, the General gallantly steering the mummy by the arm. "You'll be right as rain after a bath and change of linen. Do you like gin? Do

you play bridge? Do you go in for singing *a cappella*?"
But the mummy remains silently grim. That night while
the guests are sleeping, the defunct Egyptian (gifted with
supernatural power by Kuk, god of darkness and the
Underworld) invades the mind of Tey, adored millennia
before our common age—now, by metempsychosis, the
Chambermaid. There, it insinuates a dream in which they
are once more lying in each other's arms during the reign
of Cheops, who built the pyramid at Giza. In the morning
both have vanished. In her bed among the tumbled sheets,
we find the Mummy's bandage. At breakfast the Boatman
informs us that a swan boat is missing from the pier.
"They have returned," says the Telepath, who saw, in his
own dream, theirs, "to Aswan on the Nile to sit beneath
the date palms and watch ibis walk stiffly in the shallows,
spearing silver fishes in the sun." The Taxidermist puts
down his fork and hurries in a swan boat after them. (He
hoped with patient study to unravel the ancient mysteries
of embalming.) But he soon returns to tell us that their
dream is beyond our own. "They are in a time that
cannot be recalled by artifice—no matter how desperate
we are to have it come again." The musicians put away
their instruments, sheet music scattering in the wind.

22.

"While said to be unmusical, German has sonorities
pleasing to the ear of Germans," remarks the Prime
Minister, who relishes sauerkraut and recites at this
moment Rilke's sonnets to him—to Orpheus, slumped in
an ice-cream-parlor chair, an arm against its lyre-shaped
back, his fingers touching, as it were, the strings of it. "You
cannot hope to ransom your Eurydice from death with

relevant, unseductive songs!" the P.M. chides the ancient Greek in a language that ought not to be understood by him, but somehow is. "Threnodies for victims of earthquake, dirges for casualties of war, laments for penguins whose polar homes are shrinking are mutton to a woman in thrall to strange impulses. You must, as you did in antiquity, sing to her of indolent Thracian afternoons, of the blue sea among the Peloponnesian isles, of evenings under myrtle trees. Eurydice must be made to wake from the fatal spell woven like a shroud by Hades' hand. His fingers equal yours in nimbleness, though his voice numbs. Once, yours would bloom in her overnight as moonflowers do." Bewildered, Orpheus sits musing in the lengthening shadows (an effect of the Electrician's, whose stage artifices delight) and dibbles with a finger the chocolate mousse brought him by the Maître d'. (As if chocolate were a universal balm!) The Greek speaks at last, "I was in the underworld and, coming up the winding stairs, expected to see the ice-cold marble halls of the Palace of the Dead. Who are you?" His perplexity stirs in us sympathy for one, like us, who belongs to another time. "What race of men?" His voice ascends to a falsetto of fury to find himself so lost. "Or are you gods?" That makes us laugh! "We are mortal and the dreams of mortals. We are real and un-, here and not, affirmation and negation, yes and no, 0 and 1. Would you like a drink, cigarette, or dance ticket? There are pleasures of a kind in this hotel that make us glad we came." "But from where," asks Orpheus, "did you come?" We squirm in our chairs, wanting to forget. Only the Plumber does not hesitate to answer, having plumbed the lines of our descent: "The world." We turn our heads, ashamed or afraid or both. The world with its smoking towers, roadside bombs, greenhouse gases, poisoned earth. "Outside is death, Orpheus, and the cities of the dead!" the Chanteuse says in a voice colored by emotion. She has, like him, a gift to weld us to her breath. He rises, knocking over the chair, which jars like an unstrung lyre the sudden silence of the hotel bar. "Then maybe she is there," he says sadly. "Eurydice!" He strides toward the stairs, stops, stands uncertainly, asks: "How do I reach the world?" The Chanteuse cries, "No, Orphée, please! Stay with us!" She imagines love duets in the Aegean Room, romantic chansons sung among the ruins, and soft Lydian airs played by their two mouths' embouchures pressed one against the other. What is a General of cavalry to the son of Apollo and Calliope, whose song moved trees and stones! How impuissant even the hotel's Telepath by whose gaze a spoon can sidle across a table! "Stay, Orphée!" The Chanteuse is opening her blouse while the lights dim to simulate the lambency of hearth or forge. Suddenly a cardboard *Argo* slips across a painted ocean, sail swollen with wind. "We have the works of Pindar, Bulfinch, and Edith Hamilton. We know what is to happen, even if you do not: your death at the hands of the Maenads, your head left on Lesbos!" He listens as if to history's distant roar, sound of sea and fire. His eyes rest upon the Chanteuse, turning her throat and breasts to roses. She sings—a siren song!—and he forgets Eurydice until the orchestra wheezes into Jacques Offenbach's "Infernal Gallop" and the Funambulist on her tightrope dances the can-can, impudently showing her bloomers. "This is a farce!" the P.M. rages. Lost to us as surely as Eurydice to him, Orpheus enters the lobby mirror and his death—his disembodied head drifting down the river Hebrus, serenaded by nightingales.

23.

"We have received a distress signal from the moon," the hotel's Telegrapher announces dispassionately, reciting—in dots-and-dashes—the lunar lament (which is noise to me and would be still even were the Chanteuse to trill it). Her throat—a golden chalice—is, at this hour, being kissed by the General as they allow the evening with its soft dusk to invade them. "I do not know Morse code," I say patiently, for I fear the man's tendency to spite. "If you will kindly transliterate." But he will not and, turning on his heels, goes back upstairs to his station, furnished scantily as you would expect of someone for whom language is laconic. A silk stocking said to have belonged to Garbo is his sole concession to superfluity. I dislike him for his delight in bearing bad news to the guests. Impulsively I follow, premeditating murder with only the weapon in doubt. The piano-wire in my pocket has not been tested on a neck. The Taxidermist's reproductions of our illustrious guests—all of which I have garroted—do not count. Regardless of means, I am determined to put an end to the Telegrapher's unpleasantness, even if I confine annihilation to his digits. Vengeance, however, is confounded by a Penrose Stairs (constructed by the Carpenter, who has a fondness for M.C. Escher), which diverts the climber relentlessly away from his destination. Treads become risers during a violent torsion the staircase twists into a Möbius strip my shoelaces stand stiffly my hat falls up! Furious, I promise to murder the Carpenter, when I am overtaken by the Funambulist on her tight-rope.

"Husband, what brings you here?" I sense an opportunity for recreation. "Since you will not come down," I say, "I have come up." She sighs—resignedly, not amorously—and, after securing her balancing-pole, steps out onto a landing useless for all save love. There, we strive to persuade each other of the erotic potential of our points of view: hers aerial, mine terrestrial. Pulse and respiration returned to normal, she takes up her pole and course beneath the hotel's coffered ceilings. Cured of homicidal rage (the result evidently of prolonged abstention), I wish the world well—even the Telegrapher, whose staccato can be heard at the limit of audition (leaving me to wonder at the almost galactic distances inside this hotel). Going back the way I came leads nowhere. Despite its grand flights and elegant spirals, Penrose Stairs are a nightmare topography without exit—an elaboration of one of Oscar Reutersvärd's Impossible Objects. "Help!" I shout, wishing to be once more in the company of people— indulging, now that night has come, their appetites in the hotel bar. As if in answer, the orchestra plays an air of such desolation that I weep to hear it. "What is that melody?" I ask the Conductor, who with his orchestra has appeared on a loggia in a mist of Nothingness. "*Elegy for the Moon*," he answers. "Each of us woke with it in our minds. We cannot be rid of it, except by playing." "Who composed it?" "It seems the moon did, at least this is our impression." "It sang to you in your sleep?" I ask. "In a voice that drenched us in tears and dust." "The moon was there inside your dream?" "Its light was, which we liken to pearls or a drop of mercury or the brightness of leaves when the wind turns them to the sun." He quickens his baton, and the musicians lurch once more from silence into music, their swallow-tail coats rent with grief. In the shadows funereal figures glide on the slowly drawn bows of violins. The Funambulist returns—extraordinary to meet her twice in a single night (or age)!—and with her lance tilts me softly into bed.

24.

For his birthday the General wishes for a carrousel. Although he will not admit to such a childish desire, the Telepath has seen it in his mind—the sentimental longing for a roundabout, hidden under thoughts of saddle-trees, horse's withers, eighteenth-century military histories by Quincy, Bourcet, and Tempelhoff, and—his favorite bedtime reading—Philip St. George Cooke's *U.S. Army Cavalry Manual*. In a dragoon decorated for courage and once kissed by Marshal Foch, merry-go-rounds are shameful. "Were the world to hear of it," the General tells himself, "I would be decommissioned: ribbons and buttons torn off, saber broken, my name struck from the regimental list of all who've served with honor and distinction." The General shudders at the mere idea, for his standing in the field of military arts is dear to him as must it be to any man who has made them his career. And so he answers those among the guests he counts as friends the question of his preferences for a birthday gift: "A riding crop, curry-comb, or tin of saddle soap" (though he has no horse or saddle, nor is there saddlery or store in which to buy them). But the Telepath betrays the General's fondest wish to the Engineer and Taxidermist—not from meanness but for love, which they three bear him. So while the others apply their cunning to devise articles befitting an old horse soldier, the inseparable pair sets about to make a carrousel. The Taxidermist constructs four horses as you would a couch—horsehair wound about armatures of wood and iron, with newspapers and blankets for added girth. These he upholsters in skin or hide of animals whose genus he will not divulge in case we should feel squeamish. The effect is lifelike; they are entirely plausible as fairground horses—the type that revolves (sometimes going up and down as well) on a circular platform. It is the Engineer, who sets them going—his genius in harnessing energy such as the planetary motion of Mars, deliberately undermined by the volatility of certain gases, which he traps in scientific glassware. The resulting movement is best described as eccentric or, if one deals as mathematicians do in numbers, irrational like the $\sqrt{5}$—even surreal like a Dedekind Section. The horses go in obedience to the circularity of a carrousel, but with aberrations. A statistician would define the effect stochastic, or improbable. To describe the movement, however, is not to comprehend it. We who have tested it do not. It is as if the whole thing were a dream—like so much else in our hotel. Nevertheless, the General is delighted with his gift and would have kissed his benefactors if his militant moustache had not reminded him of his dignity at the point of contact with the Engineer's cheek. The General is not French and suffered Marshal Foch because of military etiquette! All that afternoon, we eat cake and dance the foxtrots favored by the General. In his honor, the musicians have taken caffeine extract to keep from sleeping. He acknowledges each token of respect with a grave nod of his august head, the Chanteuse demure and lissome by his side. "Thank you, friends," he says, "for this celebration of my natal day. I've marked it in encampments bitter as Caesar's in Gaul, Napoleon's at Waterloo, and Haig's at the Somme. Of all the irrealities, war is *nonpareil*," he says, eating one from a box of chocolates. "Now that I'm an old man, I realize the better part of valor is to write one's memoirs in an armchair with whiskey and tobacco at one's elbow. I might have spared myself fifty years of Spartan deprivation by making up the skirmishes in my head. I realize, furthermore, that the only horses I've ever cared for are the wooden kind of childhood. Perhaps" (he has gone on already at an uncharacteristic length) "I became a cavalry officer only to recover the joy I took in them." The General cries and wipes his eyes with a handkerchief presented—with many happy returns of the day—by the Prime Minister, his friend. We are moved and draw away while the Electrician dims the lights so discreetly you'd think night were falling. The wind-machine scatters pseudo-leaves as though an evening breeze had risen and, with it, the cries of birds (those of nocturnal habits)—a musical production of the Flautist. The room is black, the breeze is still, a silver-foiled moon suspended from the ceiling—its beams illuminate the carrousel. At last the General surrenders to his desire to ride the painted horse, whose rhythm is as familiar as breathing's. Shyly he goes and mounts it, sitting *haut* in the saddle like a young cadet. The orchestra plays Satie's "*Gymnopédie* No. 1," and the General—rapt, triumphant—circles circles until for him there is no end or beginning—only this.

25.

Studies like those by Muybridge, using the camera to record incremental movement in a horse or pugilist, fascinate the

Photographer. For him the General's carrousel is fruitful for research: how its wooden horses seem to revolve, as well as rise and fall, by means of belts and camshafts in a frenetic counterfeit of motion. Relatively-speaking, the horses do not move at all, because of a carrousel's ineluctable circularity (where to go forward is to come back). Entranced, the Photographer lingers to take a picture of this paradox, after the cake has been eaten by the guests and the General has dismounted from his painted horse. But in the darkroom while the negative is assembling its *chiaroscuro* in the bath, the Photographer makes a discovery that unnerves him: the absence of the General from the picture of the carrousel. "How is it that the roundabout is clearly there with each of the Four Horses of the Apocalypse [a joke!], but not the General?" asks the Prime Minister. The Photographer shrugs in bemusement. "Is it trick photography?" the Building Inspector wants to know. He is acquainted with chicanery, such as when a builder builds a building with only an illusion of foundation or—worse—in midair with none. Outraged, the Photographer will not stoop to answer. "It may be the carrousel that causes the General to disappear, through the medium of photosensitive emulsion struck by light," speculates the Plumber. "If the horses, say, were smeared with the contents of jelly donuts." Now it is the turn of the fabricators—Taxidermist and Engineer— to be incensed. "No!" they shout in unison. (As a rule, they are inseparable.) "Don't blame us for this oddity, which science in time will get to the bottom of." We troop upstairs *en masse* to interview the General, entertaining in his room the Chanteuse, whose voice can break glass if she wishes. Fortunately she doesn't, for there are no glazers or surplus windowpanes; and winter is by all reports bitter outside the hotel. "General, forgive this intrusion; but we would like with your permission to make certain you exist." Pulling on his clothes, the General roars— in anger or merriment, who can tell? I notice, though, how pink the Chanteuse is. Having buttoned up his tunic, the General takes an antique watch and chains it to his pants. "Might not that watch, artifact from an earlier age, account for his disappearance in the photograph?" the Plumber asks, who studied metaphysics in his youth. "While it's true, it may not keep perfect time, it binds me to the moment more or less," the General answers peevishly. "With your indulgence, sir, I should like to verify your presence by pinching you." "That won't be necessary!" the Chanteuse declares, lifting her negligee to show a pretty thigh decorated by a recent bruise. "Before you barged in (next time be kind enough to knock!), the General pinched *me*; I felt his fingers and in them the truth of his reality." "Spinoza says that the mind is just an idea of the body," the metaphysical Plumber observes. "Perhaps the terms are reversible and the body, an idea of the mind." "But if so, whose?" the P.M. shouts annoyed. He has no patience for philosophy. The Telepath, who has been gazing at the Chanteuse's knees, states categorically: "I have read the General's mind; I can read it now, though it makes me blush." The Photographer hazards the opinion that the General may, in fact, be projected by some other's. "Such an infinite recession will drive us mad!" the P.M. screams in a manner some consider shocking in a parliamentarian. But I do not, knowing to what distraction men can be driven by a conundrum beyond hope of solving. "I think we are all ghosts!"

the Chanteuse cries so that our hearts break. "O, dear General, make them go!" We do as we are told while, unheroic in his underwear, the old man comforts her. "There is nothing to be done," the P.M. says, "but to have our pictures taken. We'll know then if she is right or— as I suspect—the General's faking. Don't ask me how!" But the Photographer, bored with the supersensory, will not lend his camera to further ontological investigation. "Tonight, I take the ferry to Tibet (crossing on the lake beneath us) to watch the Roof of the World melt and make a time-lapse photograph of a glacier. My focus is on the universe, the part of it we can see, though seeing is a challenge requiring sophisticated optics and art." I wish the Photographer bon voyage and wander off in search of my wife, but she is not on any part of the high-wire perceptible to me. I am disquieted by the thought that my Funambulist, too, may be a ghost. But I feel in every nerve and pore traces her body left during our brief encounters in midair. Love is the tightrope that I walk—not without risk of falling and death.

26.

In the hotel's deepest cellar where the lake is, black mostly in that sunless underground (electric moons of every lunar hue and phase can be drawn on almost visible wires to lighten it), the Interior Designer, who once dreamed of a theatrical career like Edward Gordon Craig's, creates the Nile at the time of the Pharaohs, in particular of Cleopatra. His interest, frankly, does not lie (like mine) in her dusky thighs, ebon hair, and clavicles bisected by the straps of two precisely conical housings for the royal breasts. Properties, costumes, and stage furniture, combined into a picturesque tableau, excite him only. We are invited to the debut of this rich Ptolemaic fantasy by messengers singing *a cappella*, formerly employed by Western Union. "Gentlemen, please join us for an evening of ancient spectacle and *dishabille*, starring Cleopatra and an asp," they declaim in recitative more suitable for opera than a pantomime. Our blood is on the boil (that which flows in the men of our hotel) by the prospect even of a counterfeit Cleopatra, and we resolve to attend her after a dinner of Oysters Rockefeller. O, the never-quite-extinguished fire of men in middle-age! We go shyly—even the General, who spent a year in Egypt, bivouacked near the pyramid of Cheops—feeling like boys about to kiss girls for the first time or fumble at their breasts. The swan boats and gondolas are not at their usual moorings, replaced by a barge painted gold, rowed by thirty Nubian oarsmen manufactured by the Engineer. On a throne sit Cleopatra and a monkey—both emblematic of men's folly. "The monkey is mine!" boasts the Taxidermist, who stuffed it. We applaud him for the sake of courtesy, though we do not care overmuch for simians now that we have a nearly naked queen to feast our eyes upon. "The moment is one of high romance!" the Plumber, who is not typical of his trade, exults—enthralled by Cleopatra's elbow (reminding him of pipe). The General's eyes are fastened on her slippers in a way that makes us wonder if he is not a fetishist. Torch flames rock on the lake's agitated surface, like roseate salamanders treading water. (Or are they newts? Regardless, they are beautiful.) Transfixed by them, we find it difficult to tear our eyes away to gaze at Cleopatra, whom we came to see (not these illusory amphibians!). We do look at her at last and are captivated by forms generated by algorithms of desire. Physically she is more impressive than all the oarsmen put together. The orchestra plays a nocturne while the water sobs against the hull and the moon slides into view, suspended from a wire. "Things are going well!" declares the Decorator, and we cannot deny it. Next, we are treated to an amorous interlude during which the Queen and Marc Anthony dally on the Nile. "I am glad that, at the last minute, I decided to attend!" the Prime Minister exclaims. He was in favor of a dance instead, when he might press his pin-striped suit against a lissome body. "This is art of the first water and not the pornography I expected." In a pink spotlight, a girl walks across the beach, carrying a placard on which is written: CLEOPATRA DIES BY ASP. "But this is not historically accurate!" complains the Plumber. "Cleopatra died inside her palace." But we shush him, knowing that art observes a greater truth than realism. She presses the tiny reptile to her bosom, which is lush, and in a moment dies. We are too moved to listen to the Engineer explain how he transformed an ordinary worm-gear into an asp miraculous in movement and detail. He stalks away in high dudgeon while our hearts—riven by tragedy—urge our eyes to tears. The Decorator waits in anticipation of applause, which we withhold so overcome are we by similitude, while the monkey scuttles winningly among us, begging with his little hat for coins. But not for the world would we defile this moment by base trade. *Adieu*, monkey! *Adieu*, Cleopatra, who is sailing in her barge toward Osiris and the Underworld—all torches out, all oars shipped, and the mechanical hearts of the rowers stopped. We may never again see such a spectacle as this of Cleopatra and the Asp!

27.

When the orchestra is awake and playing *tutti* a tune we like, interruptions enrage so that, ordinarily amiable and pacific, we are liable to strike him or her or it that distracts the musicians from their music. Blood has been shed from noses, and vases (even Ming) flung across the room. We would beat our mothers were they foolishly to ask whether we wanted white sauce or raisin on our ham. Imagine then our anger when a subway train appears in the middle of the ballroom where we are dancing! To be precise, a subway *station*. We do not see the train halt beneath the dance floor. The General, nibbling a dainty ear of the Chanteuse, orders a cavalry charge—forgetting that his horses are not real. "Cannon, then! Surely there must be an artillery piece somewhere in the hotel!" "Dynamite it," the Prime Minister, who lost his office to anarchists, advises. "There's a stick in the pantry next to the Tabasco." The Maître d' is dashing there when who but the Journalist should be coming up the subway stairs, his battered Underwood pendent at his side! "I did not think to see you again in this life," sighs the Manicurist, who has carried a torch ever since his departure from the hotel. He kisses her, having missed her, too, during his sojourn in reality. "I brought you this," he says, making her a present of a flower, which is dead. Reality is hard on flowers. She will press it later in *The History of Chocolate*, commencing with the Mayans, who liked it hot and spicy. "What brought you back?" the Prime Minister inquires. "Life outside," he answers, "is all but d—" "What news of the moon?" the General rudely interposes. The Journalist takes off his hat as if in mourning. "Not good," he says. "It pines for starry night, rolling seas, and aromatic firs in whose branches it was wont to rest." "What a funny way to talk!" laughs the Building Inspector, who prefers *vox populi*. "I've been reading Shakespeare to it—the sonnets and the plays. The moon is fond of the Elizabethan Age. The present distresses it." "Do the anarchists torture it?" the General demands, his moustache bristling. "They starve it," the Journalist replies. "You would weep to see the moon, now that it is no more than a sliver of its former self." "I am appalled!" the General rages as Lear did on the roaring heath. But what good's ire in an old man good for nothing but ballroom dancing! We look away for pity's sake. The Journalist sits and says, "You may be interested to hear how the hotel appears to those outside." "Yes, we would!" the P.M. affirms. "It is something I have wondered about." "So have I!" I say. "Me, too!" the Manicurist cries for fear the Journalist has forgotten her, now that he is serious—a side of him that does not thrill her like his amorous one. "The hotel moves." "Moves?" "It shifts. It is never in any one place for long." (Proof, perhaps, of String Theory?) "And when it's moving, it blurs—sometimes disappears." (Just as the Physicist predicted!) "It is this that keeps you safe from siege. This and something also inexplicable: the building changes architectural style. When I left, it was *rococo*. Last time I looked, Art Deco." "How bizarre!" the Building Inspector remarks. "It is sheer luck that I am here at all, though I wished to be." The Journalist lays his eyes on the Manicurist, who blushes. "How so?" the P.M. asks, intrigued. "The hotel came to rest atop the subway platform at the exact moment my train stopped. The conjunction is accidental and brief." As if on cue, we perceive the unseen train depart by a screech of steel and an odor of ozone. The stairs leading down disappear as we shuttle block by block across the city—up, down, and sideways like a rook in chess—scarcely visible to our enemies, inside the bastion of our hotel.

28.

And if, as I sometimes think, the hotel is all my own devising—why have I not equipped myself by a willful act of imagination with a sac such as birds have? With it I might ascend—dreaming—to my Funambulist and, after ceremonies of love, join her on the high-wire beneath the ceiling (festooned with trapezes of dust as if to remind us that life can be a circus, though there are no elephants). I would not wish for feathers—would not be a bird-man (a being, like us, preferring life in between). I would, however, be a cowboy like those I saw in movies during a childhood deprived of cows—drinking bitter coffee under lonesome skies while tumbleweed and prairie schooners drive before the wind. So I rustle, with the Plumber's help, the General's horses while he is on sabbatical with his Chanteuse in a cabin by the lake—there, to study the nuptial customs of mechanical swans. Having unhitched the horses from the carrousel, we ride across the High Sierra Room, through a plaster-of-Paris pass—horses buried to their knees in Ivory Snow—and after days of hardship, onto a plain created by the Decorator from bolts of felt meant to cover snooker tables. In town I leave the Plumber to water our horses (thirsty, though they are mostly wood) while I take off my spurs in a room above the gaudiest saloon. Like any other cowboy in the company of animals and gruff, unshaven men, I long for a woman. So I telegraph downstairs for one, and in no time up comes the Hat-Check, dressed in cowgirl skirt and vest, smoking a cheroot. "Are you happy in this dream?" I ask her, "or would you rather have a different one?" She is about to answer when my wife's face in the windowpane reminds us that I am not at liberty to dally with cow- or any other kind of girls. Sheepishly I smile at my acrobatic bride while the Hat-Check does up the buttons of her blouse. In the saloon below, the Prime Minister, playing the role of the Hanging Judge, is looking at a catalogue of rope. Surly and dyspeptic, he hankers to stretch a neck or two before day dwindles to a close. The guests applaud the fidelity of his acting, overlooking the skimpiness of his false moustache. The General with the Chanteuse on his arm abruptly enters through the swinging-door. The P.M.'s moustache would have twirled in his surprise if the mucilage had not been Peerless. "We did not expect you two so soon!" "The swans were misbehaving," the General comments. "Passing by the carrousel, I noticed my horses have been stolen." "What's that you say?" The Hanging Judge is all *en point*. "Stolen? Horse theft's a hanging crime!" He is pleased to have a thing to set his mind on; life in the Old West is often boring. A vigilante mob of three drags in the Plumber, whose hair looks like a magpie's nest, after napping in the stable's stall. "String him up!" the P.M. shouts, breaking his gavel on the desk. "No, not me!" the Plumber cries. "Norman was the mastermind!" "Where's he now?" the Judge demands with all the majesty he can muster. "In the room upstairs with his fancy woman," the Manicurist, in the role of preacher's wife, informs the court. "Let's hang 'em!" shouts the Engineer in town on railroad business. "Not before he pays his bill!" the Barman begs. "When you're finished, may I stuff him?" asks the Taxidermist, who has been complaining of a scarcity of subjects for his art. "Help!" I call as the town's folk thunders up the stairs with murder in its heart, which in a mob is a single sanguinary organ. The Cowgirl faints, but I have no time to take advantage of her state. They are breaking down the door! It is nearly splintered when Quasimodo shambles through my window, crying: "Sanctuary!" Nimble as a tightrope-walker, he tiptoes—high above the dusty street—toward Notre Dame Cathedral while, like a sack of spuds, I hang across his misbegotten shoulder. Where did he learn the art of funambulism and—of even greater interest—how did this Hunchback, who should be in Medieval France, arrive in 1880's Kansas? Who is dreaming this? Someone who has seen too many movies! A thought can sometimes splinter in a brain undermined by cocktails and lingerie (or even stamps if one happens to overindulge a passion for philately) with havoc the result. I only hope that—tottering above an abyss of multiplying fantasies—I will be upheld by Quasimodo until he sets me down to rest among the gargoyles and sorority of bells.

29.

for Kathryn Rantala

Where all is only words, why not a menagerie? Write the word ELEPHANT. Now LION. Now TIGER. And DOG wearing a skirt and hat, balanced on a ball. And SEAL with a ball balanced on its nose. I might with practice endue them with motility or, if unable to create an organism so advanced, move them—as the Telepath does spoons—across a space of beaten earth. He sends spoons sliding across the table, but the principle is the same. Words are counters of the mind playing "a simple game I made up in the dark" as Raymond Queneau said of literature. Outside is a dark and moonless age, and so I came to live in this hotel—to be away a while from the grave. The Cigarette-Girl, who wished for a circus, is glad. "Thank you, Norman, for this dream!" I bow, and my ringmaster's hat topples toward my boots anchored in the center-ring. Quicker than the movement of desire, she seizes it before its black silk has even grazed the ground (despite gravity's peremptory summons) and with a little broom whisks it clean of hypothetical dust. Her eyes say to me, "I will do anything to please you for this gift!" I am about to embrace her when the Funambulist's stern shadow scythes between us. It is always so in my dreams: no sooner do I take a woman in my arms than my tightrope-walking wife tiptoes into view. "Not even during wishful thinking is infidelity allowed!" I shout, aggrieved. The Engineer looks up from his elegant diagram of a trapeze "that will defy death!" to remark on the Shepherdess in whose company I can be found when my aerialist is in her apogee. "She belongs to pastoral literature; our trysts are fictional!" I am defensive, admittedly. "We are drinking cocktails in honor of the musicians," the General announces with the suavity of someone used to wearing epaulettes. The Engineer—his mind a planisphere shining with equations—criticizes his intemperance. "The Barman's donated a jar of pickled onions," the General continues with the relish of an epicure. "Won't you join us?" "First, Norman must finish my circus!" objects the girl who sells tobacco products. The General waves her kisses with his fingertips, then thrusts a tiny sword into an onion. He broke his grownup's one across his knee to pacify the Chanteuse, who prefers torch songs to threnodies. He shuts the door on the barroom's yellow light, leaving us to our devices. "Your animals are nicer than the Taxidermist's," the young girl says to flatter me. "Please write me a monkey." And I do—a green one from Senegal, for words are generous and by their incantation do we live in hiding during a monstrous age.

30.

What excitement! The Director, who arrived "like a god" one afternoon on a piece of stage machinery lowered from the roof, will reenact *Ben-Hur*. The Palatine Hill, where Romulus and his brother Remus were mothered by a wolf, is nearly finished. Below it, remarkable reproductions of Roman barges ply a model Tyrrhenian Sea. "The Decorator has outdone himself!" the Soubrette praises. "Yes," the Prime Minister agrees, "his Circus Maximus is a masterpiece." We tremble to hear the pawing of Arabian steeds! Foaled by nightmares, they are confined in a corral warranted to withstand earthquakes and their aftershocks of 7 on the Richter Scale. Inspired by their terrible neighing, the Chanteuse trills *Cantata for Equus*. "And who," the General asks, "is to be Ben-Hur, the Hebrew charioteer?" The Prime Minister, whose judgment is unclouded by sentiment or graft, nominates the Plumber. Indignant, the General rings his cavalry spur in protest, against a fluted column. "Only hands used to monkey-wrenches are strong enough to hold the reins," the P.M. states. Blustering, the General reminds us of his equestrian exploits on a hill in Cuba. "That was long ago!" the P.M. snaps, and we detect a note of malice glittering like a scimitar's sharpened edge. "Pish!" the old man sputters. "You shall play the part of Tiberius," the P.M. says, relenting. "The Roman Emperor?" "None other." How the General beams to have been accorded such an honor! "But I don't have a toga, or is that just for Greeks?" "There are hampers brimming with costumes from every period," says the Soubrette, who for the nonce is acting as Costumier. The General claps his hands and hurries off. "Who is to play Messalah and race his chariot against Ben-Hur's?" inquires the Historian in his capacity as technical adviser. "Norman." "No, I'm out of shape and easily tired!" I protest. "Hmmmm. What about the Carpenter?" the Decorator suggests. "He's brawny and unafraid of horses." "Yes, a fine idea!" The day arrives for which we have been waiting. The circus seats are crowded. The guests, attired picturesquely like first century *Anno Domini* Roman citizens, are eating hotdogs and drinking beer in paper cups. Despite a reputation as a tyrant on the set, the Director is unable to forbid anachronisms such as these, as well as a musical score played on modern instruments. Anticipating blood and mayhem, the hotel Physician is ecstatic. There is little to occupy a man of his profession when sickness and injury are virtually extinct. I sit by the Shepherdess, who looks suitable to any age, and admire the Roman maidens in their *décolletage* while on the Tiber galley slaves contend with currents flustered by a wind-machine. Now, a fanfare is blaring in the cyclorama's cloudless sky. The Emperor drops a handkerchief and, when it has finished fluttering to the rutted track, the race begins. Four chariots leap and rattle down the lanes, pulled by horses whipped to fury. Obedient to the oval, the chariots orbit until there are only two that interest us: Ben-Hur's and his former friend Messalah's, whose wheels are equipped with turning blades! He hopes with them to dismantle the Jew's, which lacks accessories. In spite of them, Ben-Hur's enemy tumbles from his chariot. The Physician rushes to his mangled side, a smile on his lips; and with instruments once used by his father for tending duellers, practises his healing art on the Roman, who, notwithstanding, dies. A shadow, scarcely noticed, has been crawling across the churned and bloody sand. Aware of it at last, I think it cast by a vulture or other bird of death—a finale provided by the Director for his spectacle. But looking up, I see my tightrope-walking wife, passing loftily over Circus Maximus. She ignores the kiss I throw her, doubtlessly annoyed by the Shepherdess at my side. "She means nothing!" I shout. But the high-wire artiste, who has renounced the ground, does not stop to answer.

31.

The Fireman set fire to the Roman Room where the Violinist moonlights as Nero while the other musicians are asleep or in rehearsal. He is first chair of all the strings and needs none. "This arson is not the work of an authentic pyromaniac," the Analyst concludes. "That is, one consumed by notions of holocaust, which is, psychically speaking, an erotic contagion devouring what is touched. The Fireman's delight, however, is alchemical as he watches baser material alter into a gold and ruby conflagration." "He is, notwithstanding, a danger to us all!" retorts the Prime Minister, whose view is of the commonweal. "He must be apprehended, and his head cut off." "But he is our friend!" the Chanteuse cries.

She has been keeping company with the Fireman behind the General's back because of the former's ardor, which is larger than that of the old man, whose moustache droops. But the P.M. is adamant in his resolve to arrest the "firebug" before the hotel is rendered unfit to live in. The Engineer and the Decorator, whose interests are antithetical, argue the possibility—each from his own entrenched position—of burning to the ground an imaginary structure. Indifferent, I compose a tribute to my Funambulist bride, whose ankles have just come into view. "Look!" shrieks the Masseuse, pointing in alarm to real smoke on the painted horizon. "The palm trees are ablaze!" They are papier-mâché. "Whom do you suppose could have disabled the sprinklers?" the Building Inspector inquires. As if in answer, the Fireman sidles from the scene with a canister of gasoline. Happily the elephants (whose existence has been doubtful) shamble from the Serengeti Room and with their muscular trunks, having first unlimbered them, douse the flames with water brought for the purpose from a puddle on the plain. "Elephants are not so dumb as they pretend!" says the Prime Minister, who reprises then his punitive theme: "I sentence the Fireman to be chained to a rock in the Gibraltar Room—there, to be pecked at daily by an eagle." (Miracle of the Taxidermist's art.) "But this is wrong!" the Historian shouts. "The mythic figure to which you allude was chained to Mt. Caucasus: I speak, of course, of the titan Prometheus, who stole the gods' fire in a fennel stalk and for this impudence was—" "Yes, yes, we have read Bulfinch!" the Plumber, who is Classical in his methods and approach to pipes, snarls. The Designer is delighted with the sentence, seeing in the fettered Fireman a way to finish the room's looming piece of Jurassic limestone, which in his opinion is "too much of a good thing." "May I visit him?" the Masseuse asks between (or is it amid?) sobs. "At twilight to distract him," the P.M. answers. "In this way, his flammable fancy will be less likely to catch fire from the setting sun's example." "I shall take him cakes and oranges and massage his aching back and be to him a wife such as the Funambulist is to you." She looks at me in recognition of the impediment to union imposed by my wife's aerial vocation. "And I shall play for you and your Fireman a fiery—" "No, no, not fiery!" interjects the Prime Minister. "Are you mad?" The Violinist recants: "Forgive my thoughtlessness. I shall play for them a single soothing note on my brightest string." "The hotel has become something less than a utopia," the P.M. laments. "Art and love, however, have conspired to restore order to our disordered system—a triumph for Chaos Theory!" As if to mock the vanity of human certitude, a meteor hisses hotly through the hotel atmosphere (singeing the flounce on my beloved's acrobatic attire). "Great balls of fire!" cries the General. "No one is safe until the Fireman is found and taken into custody!" A second meteor, accompanied by derisive laughter, rains incandescent debris on us. "He shall be taken and put to death!" the P.M. declares, rising up in the full majesty and great huff of his office. Thus the idea of death, which was banished, is admitted to the hotel and our dreaming. (We do not count Messalah, who is Biblical and subject to dispute by agnostics.) The maniacal Fireman, the origin of whose disease is not known, escapes his destruction in a swan boat. He goes outside where fire is ample—in a world mad for burning.

32.

Theoretical science has disturbed the aplomb of the guests, whose insouciance is less now that they know the hotel and all in it are hurtling to no purpose while vibrating spatially in twenty-six dimensions. If it were not for my Funambulist, who moves overhead like an unswerving planet, I, too, would feel uncertainty's rising damp. "You are my lodestar, my compass needle, my railroad timetable!" I shout as she passes. I gaze fondly at her ribboned underpants, recalling my nuptial visit on the high-wire she never leaves, wishing—as I do always—that she would live on the ground like me. But her clay and destiny are different from mine (quite possibly from all others'), and I pay her homage, which she acknowledges by tipping her balancing-pole before tottering into the darkness at the end of the wire. Her departure is propitious, for a chaotic weather pattern at this moment wreaks havoc in the Sahara Room where we are eating figs. "The camels!" the Taxidermist shouts, too late to save them. (They are tedious to stuff.) The caravansary is also carried off, together with yoghurt and burnooses. "Run!" the General, who was in Arabia with Lawrence, commands—mouth full of sand in spite of his moustache, which ought to have strained it. Now the oasis is under attack—its papier-mâché palms torn to shreds by the burnishing wind! Ours—we later learn— was not the sole meteorological quirk. Snow fell on the Côte d'Azure Room, surprising several nudists, and *föhn*, familiar on the lee side of the Alps, drove one of our most ebullient to suicide. (By luck or prowess, my aerial bride escaped all harm.) The Prime Minister has denounced the Meteorologist for malfeasance in permitting such conditions to develop unforeseen and for the loss of his toupee. The House Detective's report confirms our worst suspicion: "The Meteorologist was drunk. He fed the weather simulator with choreography. Only the application of my blackjack saved us from the *lambada*, which was next." "That would have been catastrophic!" the Engineer declares. "The hotel walls will not withstand dances of the South American sort." The Analyst, tugging at his beard, avers: "Neither will our soles." This abysmal pun, not even Freud would have countenanced, though he might have cited it in *Jokes and Their Relation to the Subconscious*. "I adore the dithyrambic!" sighs the Hairdresser, demonstrating the *fandango* with her heels and fingers' castanets. The Journalist arrives as if from out a grave. "What's wrong?" the House Detective asks, seeing tragedy written in his face. "Come see," his terse reply. We follow him down the winding metal stairs to the cellar, where the Hydrologist has been digging a canal. There, as if the water were a bed, lie bodies tossing in the feeble light of oil lamps. "Victims of the enemies of the moon," the Journalist declares. He opens the mouth of one, and we see—like a communion wafer—a white circle on the tongue left by the assassins of poetry, lunacy, and love. The musicians play *"Clair d'lune"* and weep, as do we all.

33.

Despite the hotel's feints and tendency to vanish, the virus of the quotidian gets inside it—by what method of transmission no one can say with certainty. "Perhaps the walls are like a porous membrane," the Physicist attempts an explanation. Incensed, the Building Inspector thunders that the walls are sound. "I examined them with a fine-tooth comb!" He produces the comb from his pocket "as evidence." "That's mine!" the General whines. "The curry-comb with which I groom my hobbyhorses! Give it back!" Grumbling, the Building Inspector does. "The walls are solid," he says sullenly. "Nothing—not a straw, not a glint of light can penetrate." "But you have no conception of the chasms that lie between particles bound together by the Strong Force," the Physicist says with irritating smugness. "Look, a bear dancing by the fernery!" the Cigarette-Girl exclaims. She has wished more than once for a circus or, at the very least, a zoo. Hotel life, while often amorous, can leave one between bouts yearning for something else to do. "One need only look at it," the Plumber states, "to know that a bear cannot squeeze through matter's interstices, no more than a camel through a needle's eye." He is a Baptist as you might expect of one whose working life is spent with water. "There's something strange about this bear," the General (an observer, for the Allied Powers, of the Russian Revolution) muses: "Once, when I was in the Kremlin, I watched it waltz with Isadora Duncan. I recognize the red nail polish Lenin painted on its claws." The Manicurist is intrigued by this. "What are you suggesting?" the Prime Minister asks the General. "That I may be dreaming it, the bear—or did, and now it has somehow managed to achieve its own reality." The P.M.'s response reveals an empirical nature: "Pinch it and see if it disappears." "O, I would not pinch a bear!" the Manicurist cries alarmed; "not even an illusory one. Even figments of the imagination can startle and cause the heart to stop." The bear lumbers elsewhere; the Manicurist is relieved. "I am feeling not at all myself," the General says, mopping his brow with a pink handkerchief ridiculous in a military man, no matter how superannuated. It belongs to the Chanteuse, with whom he dallies in the afternoon. "I fear we cannot keep out the outside," the P.M. sighs. We forgive him his defeatest mood—so heavily on his narrow shoulders weigh the burdens of our governance. "It is a sickness with a pathogenesis we cannot fathom or resist," he concludes. "It will enter where it wishes." "Care to join me for a cocktail on the promenade?" This, from the Physicist, whom I dislike. Thirst, however, overrules aversion, and I reply: "Why not?" We descend the iron stairs that spiral ever deeper to the cellar where the black lake is that washes on its further shore the foundations of the Paris Opera House. Half way down, the way is blocked by rocks; but they are styrofoam creations of the Decorator's, whose new interest is in ruins provided they are picturesque. "Look!" the Physicist exclaims, pointing with amazement to a dark and threatening sky. Cumbrous altocumulus clouds are rolling in from France—their charcoal linings shot with coppery incandescence. "That lightning's real!" the Physicist cries. Derisive laughter crackles out the speaker from which, as a rule, soughing wave and birdsong issue: sound effects for lake. That laugh—I swear!—belongs to the Meteorologist (now the hotel Maniac). The laugh reprises, drowned by sudden pelting rain and thunder. We take shelter in a cabana where other guests stand shivering. But this is not the last of it! A giant made of mud is shambling where waves dash on sand. "Help! The Mud Man, which I made for fun, shuddered into life when a bolt of lightning struck its earthen occiput!" The Hydrologist is screaming like a man about to lose his soul for delving into things he shouldn't. "My Mud Man's now a Golem—run!" We do while the monster jabbers in a tongue that may be Aramaic or something more autochthonous. Possessed of superhuman strength, it wreaks havoc on the promenade, finishes my gin and tonic, then vomits on the Turkish carpet. What a filthy beast! What terror to have been loosed upon our world! "We do not blame you!" we shout to the hysterical Hydrologist as we hurry up the stairs. "It's the Meteorologist's fault for meddling with the weather." In destruction's aftermath and the dispatch of the Golem with a fire hose, we are more disposed to sympathy and dictate to the Journalist a moderated view: "The Meteorologist was infected by malevolence. God knows who among us can resist! We only wonder if the episode may not be a harbinger of worse to come." The Photographer visits, with his Hasselblad, the scene of so much recent bedlam. I go with him, wanting mud (if any Golem should persist) to remind me of reality—its gall and tempests. "How long until the next breach in fantasy threatens to undo us?" Rapt in his dream, the Photographer does not see the bear admiring its claws.

34.

The Decorator is mired in a Slough of Despond. "It is on the order of Pilgrim's in Bunyan's allegory of—shall we call it 'Doubt' to be modern?" This, from the drunken Theologian between draughts of the Queen's Own. Disliking Bunyan for his dullness, I think instead of Lewis Carroll (by mind's unaccountable transits)—of his Walrus, who with a carpenter ate the gullible oysters. Innocence is soon devoured—with vinegar and salt for savor: a lesson that should be taught all tender things. "What is his sorrow?" I ask the Hat-Check, who found the would-be suicide with a noose tied round his neck. The rope was ornamental and sundered no sooner was the chair kicked over. "He has seen the Void!" replies the General with a shudder—charming in one who has stood knee-deep in slaughter. "An unfinished space is terror to a person enthralled by fabrics, rugs, and drapes!" the Analyst avers between bites of a banana. Later, I take a bouquet of artificial flowers to the suite where the Decorator lies in an agitated state after having seen what few have, in actuality. He admires them for their likeness to the real thing. "I was scraping paper from the walls— uncovering, like an archaeologist, deposits of the past. Beneath gray and vermilion stripes, I discovered (layer upon layer) galleons and pirates by N.C. Wyeth, sepia clouds and aeroplanes commemorating Lindbergh's flight, Edouard Muller's *Le Jardin d'Armide*' printed in Paris, Blondel's naughty confection '*Les Amours de Psyché*,' and Chinese paper panels with birds on twigs. All absolutely delightful, for I do not subscribe to Eastlake's opinion that 'a wall should be decorated after a manner which will belie neither its flatness nor its solidity.' Some water please?" I give him some. "Have you ever seen a more bombastic jug?" he carps. Then, returning to his theme, his face pales. "What is it?" I ask. "After having scraped the last layer of civilization from the wall, I unearthed dirt." "Dirt?" "Behind the plaster and lath: a cave with broken jars, the drawing of a horse, then stone, and after that—" "What?" "Dead space." He wraps his kimono tighter round him as if feeling again that cold surpassing any earthly chill when the stars have stalled—their fires out—and the musicians, hands stilled, regard the silent and unending night.

35.

We will give a concert for the moon! "What happiness for it!" the Cigarette-Girl cries. She is a sentimentalist with heart of gold as well she should be, here, where all is as we like it! Outside, she might not be so nice—her life's course diverted by genetic inheritance or environment or late Capitalism and a lack of suitable employment. The hotel hasn't an economist to explain how the velocity of money and the deficit conspire in the world's unhappiness. I argue that hotel life is real enough for us, though we have no economy except an exchange of pleasure—duty-free and generous. But instead of digressing, let's discuss the concert the musicians have been planning for the moon, captive still to hate. The Engineer has built an amplifier inside the observatory abandoned years before by the Astronomer. (Or was it days? Time's topology is an unraveling cloud or the fingers of a glove.) "How does the work progress?" asks the General, who adores the moon for its light, which in the darkness transfigured fields of slaughter into gardens of delight. "I am calculating Gopt." "Gopt?" "Impedance of the noise-optimizing source." "Is that necessary?" The Engineer, peering superciliously from the ladder's topmost rung, replies that he would not do so otherwise. "My amplifier will convey sonic nuance down to the hemidemisemiquaver. There will be nothing like it in the universe!" The Engineer is ordinarily not so pompose. "Yes, but will it be loud?" the General asks, vexed by the other's disdain, which he does not fail to notice. "General, it will wake the dead." "Good show!"

Down below, the orchestra rehearses a lunar *legatto*. It will be succeeded in the program by a nocturne, followed by Beethoven's "Moonlight Sonata." In addition, Baron Franz von Paula Gruithuisen's *Discovery of Many Distinct Traces of Lunar Inhabitants* (published in Munich, in 1824) has been set to music. The Chanteuse will sing the part of *Mondstrahl*. The Decorator is at work on the city Gruithuisen observed on the lunar surface through his telescope; the Taxidermist, on a herd of mooncalves and a colony of bats. "It will be spectacular!" the Journalist promises in the Arts & Culture section of Sunday's *Hotel News*—an *éclat* to rival the Taxidermist's recreation of Annie Oakley and her horse. "But will the moon be able to hear the music if the hotel's moving?" the Manicurist wants to know. (And rightly so, for that is the purpose of our effort!) The Engineer replies, "Without a doubt. I've used the latest in circulating decimal points. Even in its prison, the moon will hear it." The Manicurist cheers, for she—like all of us—mourns the moon's abduction and mistreatment. (She also has a special fondness for the moon, which rises pinkly on her clients' nails.) Some believe the music will make the satellite smile, turning up its luminosity enough to burn down the trolley barn around it. The concert is indeed sensational! The Engineer regales us with a lighting plot duplicating the effect of every lunar phase: new, quarters, crescents, both waning and waxing gibbous. At the second full moon, the Funambulist silently passes overhead on her high-wire, shedding blue light like a benediction on the floor below. For an encore of a serenade in an orchestration for harp and strings, the room is dimmed to darkness almost visible. We dance in one another's arms while revolving particles of a radiance once thought to drive men mad (and also women, for lunacy is not the prerogative of any gender) cover us—our faces foiled with joy.

36.

I stand agape with love to see my tight-rope-walking bride pursue, aloof, her solitary way beneath the ballroom ceiling where tobacco smoke is coiling like the serpent pair around Laocoön, the Greek. I envy smoke its lecherous offering to this modern Venus, whose transit resembles that other's in Aries—my sign. "I promised you an epithalamium!" I shout through the megaphone of my cupped hands from my groundling's low estate. (I mean to say I'm on the floor with the hotel's other guests washed up like flotsam after storm.) "Your language is ridiculously ornate!" the General mocks because he knows the pain of life lived starkly on history's wintry fields. But we must have poetry, no matter how inept— especially in an era such as this, when the moon has been hijacked from the heavens, her transcendent light packed into a trolley barn. "General," I say, "I'm sorry for my frailty." He clicks his tongue in answer, smiles, and kisses his Chanteuse, who—being by his side—is comfort while mine is out of reach above me. "Come down!" I cry to her, "and let me hold you. I'm old and afraid of loneliness." "I am already by your side," she answers—her voice inside my head. "I have always been. Only in your mind am I here on this rope—a Funambulist." I turn my head quickly as if to surprise that other world always just beyond vision's reach (bliss or death, who knows?) and see nothing but the empty air. "Can she be right?" I ask the General; but he has gone to bed with his sweet girl.

Why must I see only shadows? I wonder. "You are what you are," tautologically replies the Telepath, having read my mind. "Nothing can alter you." "Nothing?" "Only on a Penrose Stair or some other of your Impossible Objects can you grasp her." I weep, knowing what he says of me is true: I am disabled in the world of living men and women. "Only this—" I say, surveying with a hand my nutshell kingdom. "Only this is mine." The Funambulist sighs and, murmuring to good St. Jude a prayer for me, teeters off between her balancing-pole—an aerialist in the heart's high realms. "Yes!" says the Telepath, affirming my desire for a gin and tonic before I even thought it. (He knows a little the future—that much of it which I, who am partially omniscient, allow him.) We do not hurry to the hotel bar, knowing with certainty that, where all else is provisional, liquor isn't. The orchestra—awake—obliges with *Andante Cantabile* by Tchaikovsky. I tell myself that I am myself again. Tomorrow, I shall write another story, though it—like the stars—decorates Nothing. "The stars look handsome against the night," the Telepath says as if in answer to the question: "Why?"

37.

I wander among props and furnishings, touching them as if they were the bones of the world. Realer they are, I think to myself, than the things they mean. Papier-mâché objects painted to trick the eye into believing they are column, fountain, balustrade—they seem left over from the invention of time; their dust, dust's remnant from the original dressing of stone. "It is Prospero's palace in Sienna," the Director whispers as if reading from a playbill to someone beside him what the scene depicts, in the sudden hush before the lights are dimmed. "Beyond, the moonlit hills, the cypress trees clotted with silver— are they not magnificent? Would not the Prince himself mistake them for Tuscany's?" "Perhaps if he were drunk on wine or beauty," mocks the General, who is not— as a rule—cynical. But his Chanteuse lies upstairs in her sickbed. "It is not plague," he says. "Pray God it be not the plague!" he cries. "You are confused, my dear General," the Director says soothingly. "Only in my play does the plague rage—in my *Masque of the Red Death*." "Ah!" Stricken, the General collapses onto the counterfeit marble stairs. Its first flight announces grandeur: the landing is hung with ancestral portraits. But the second flight, which vanishes beyond the gallery wall, has been left unfinished. "Is it to stop an old man's heart that you have taken the plague for your dramatic subject when my Chanteuse is sick with a mysterious fever?" "It is a metaphor for the contagion of the Outside, which will—like a fatal brume—find us out no matter how we hide in our hotel," replies the Director, who in the world drank coffee with Brecht. "I despise Realism," the General wheezes, lacking breath to shout. "I want fables without morals—fantasies without subtext." "*Shhh!*" the Director admonishes. "The actors are ready to rehearse!" The Prime Minister in the role of the Prince declaims: "*Who dares insult us with this blasphemous mockery? Seize him and unmask him*!" "The P.M. makes a first-rate Prospero!" admires the General, whose face is no longer blue. "As a young man in the parliaments of the Empire, he must have learned to act." The General has stretched himself out upon the stair to sleep. He does and snores. I am about to kick him when the Director forestalls my boot, saying the snores will enhance the play. "They will be construed as a wind that blows the pestilence over the Prince's walls or else a trope for reason's sleep. The modern plague is not a mist of microbes squeezing through keyholes, but systemic disorder." "I think it is words," I say with an anger I do not understand. I think it is words which plague. I think I am sick at heart at having been so long shut up with them! I should like to hear a bird. "Those of the Engineer and Taxidermist are marvelous in their ingenuity," the Telepath says; "their songs, enchanting!" He draws me apart by my sleeve. I shake off his hand and with my head shake off the notion of mechanical birds. "Real birds!" I shout. "*Shhh*!" the Director adjures me to silence for his play's sake. "Maybe it's the sky behind the bird I miss. A distant sky, not projected on a cyclorama. A horizon impossible to cross." "Talk to the Analyst," the Telepath urges. "Each of us has, at one time or another, felt a panic, we are, it can seem like, it is as if we were walled up, immured, but Outside, for us, is, I assure you, death, see the Analyst, his couch, the Talking Cure, or lie down with a girl, in this state you are a danger to us all." Is there no escaping logomania? He answers my thought: "Not where all is words." I see them—words, theirs, mine—tumbling in torrents into the space within, submerging everything in pulp, in papier-mâché. "Someone turned the Fibonacci Generator on!" shouts the Engineer, hurrying onstage among the actors. "Algebraic surfaces are filling up with lattice points according to the Diophantine Equation!" I look across the footlights: the stage is a mob of Prime Ministers the cypress trees crowding the multiplying hills the moon undergoing lunar meiosis—every stage property is mirroring itself while the musicians play Bartók's *Music for Strings, Percussion, and Celesta*. Only Nothingness, over which a nearly infinite number of stairways arch, does not replicate itself; for Nothingness is Zero and therefore absolute. How attractive are nullity and void when one's self is helplessly dividing into troops! I shut my eyes and, in utter darkness where all is always only one, I hide.

38.

Secretly we wish for an Ice Age. It is not annihilation we seek but silence. Our ears ring with the din of history. Its shouts and detonations reach us even here, inside a hotel propelled through civic space by an algorithm of desire. We break down the door to the hat-check room and find our homburgs, porkpies, and fedoras changed into fur hats reminding us of cats making themselves small. Ears muffled against weather and orchestral arabesques, we revolve in disgruntlement wanting—in winter's absolutism—an end to decoration. "Come see my glacier!" announces the Engineer, voice strained through the loudspeaker's sieve. "That should be an austere sight to cheer us in our labyrinth!" exclaims the hotel's Carpenter, whose hands even now smell of pine. "But how," the Prime Minister inquires, "are we to keep from freezing in our summer clothes?" "Try these, gentlemen, if you please." The Coatroom Attendant (formerly, costumier for Ziegfeld's Follies) appears with a rack of raccoon coats. "Now we're prepared for tundra chill!" we say, stuffing ourselves into them while the suddenly naked hangers tremble. Like animals we shamble down to the wintry cellar where, only the day before, the lake was mobbed by gondoliers singing barcaroles under an artificial sun. "See how the birds, having nearly adjourned their shadows' meeting with the earth, are glazed!" the Decorator observes. "How the pier, where yesterday musicians played a serenade for mermen and -women, is swathed in snow! And how like a tongue of ice the lake is, which laps on its farther shore the cellars of the Paris Opera House!" "It travels on rollers," the Engineer explains with a charming lack of vanity. The General sings his praises from beneath the frosted handles of a cavalry moustache: "To think he did it in a single night!" "Please admire my arctic animals!" implores the Taxidermist, envious of the Engineer's acclaim. Besides polar bears, other stuffed fauna such as arctic fox, lemming, walrus, otter, and angora goats have been arranged—with superb artistry—on the moraine. "There oughtn't to be goats!" objects the Plumber, who like all who have to do with mire is a realist. "They're left over after furnishing the Arcadian Room with props," the Taxidermist snarls, incensed by the absence of applause. I remember them from an evening I played the shepherd's game with a girl in rustic skirt and blouse. Their bleating distracted me during the unlacing of her camisole. "If I were you, I'd remove the goats from an otherwise faultless *mise-en-scène*," the Plumber persists. The P.M. is inclined to agree; he, too, lacks a theatrical imagination. "Goats are incongruous!" he snorts, forming three icy clouds with his mouth and nostrils. "What is that distant reverberation?" the General asks, grizzled head cocked for overtures of tragedy. "An orchestral simulation of an avalanche," the spectacle's Director replies. "O, well done, musicians!" the General cries, eyes welling as he recalls how—long ago in the Khyber Pass—the regimental band's pipes and drums echoed. Overcome, he lies down in the ersatz snow. The P.M. wants to know if it is cold. "It is only thought that makes it so," the Director answers. "The impressionable can turn blue and, if left unattended, lose a finger or a toe." "Sometimes I long to have the real world back again!" the Maître d' exclaims. "It is incompatible with men and women," the P.M. asserts. "It is hostile to magic and art," the Director maintains. "It is death," the Carpenter declares, having made coffins in the world before arriving where death is nearly banished. "You cannot imagine how much of it there is!" In sympathy the orchestra begins a threnody, which in the twenty-seventh measure is interrupted by our shouts. "What's that on the glacier, shambling like something that's got out of a slaughterhouse (which the French pronounce *abattoir*) before its throat was cut?" the Plumber wonders for us all. "It is the modern Prometheus," replies the General, whose grandfather on Lake Constance once kissed Mary Shelley. "Frankenstein?" "His monster, yes." "And what world does it come from?" the Carpenter asks. "The real one or one like ours?" "What begins in fiction can become real and vice versa," I remark, opening my mouth to speak, whose jaw like a rusted hinge creaks from disuse. "Then he's dangerous," the P.M. concludes, "and should be put to death. For if he has escaped the world for fiction, he may infect us with the contagion of reality. Or if he is a fiction on its way to becoming real, he may denounce us to the world we have renounced." "It is a dilemma," the Plumber remarks, "from which there is no way out. The monster having once been admitted, death is ineluctable." "My dogs would tear him to pieces!"

avers the Taxidermist, whose art—like life—embraces the bestial and the beautiful. "Let us go back upstairs, gentlemen!" the General shouts above the noise of history in whose toils we are once more caught. "There, to forget in the arms of women what to remember will make us— what's the phrase?—mad as hatters!" Shivering (in fear or cold, who knows?), we hasten toward illusion.

39.

I am playing the shepherd's game by the secret lake, beneath a cyclorama on which—suitable to the evening hour—the blue of afternoon is deepening to plum while— one by one—stars appear according to a lighting scheme designed by the Electrician. When in the world, he lit the stage for Max Reinhart and other directors of German Expressionism. "Life is an illusion," I tell the Shepherdess, my hand rummaging in her blouse. "How wonderful for the living!" she replies. Light fades toward the darkest register and, with the coming of night, a manufactured breeze agitates the surface of the lake. The water lifts and settles its hem, rattling the white and nearly yellow stones. Distracted, my eyes leave hers and stray to the tiny bays coiling among stiff reeds along the shore. There, I see a bottle—its neck strangled by *Phragmites australis*, or common wetlands weed. Neither of us is surprised to find in it a message (we are living in a dream, or a play that may be comic or prove to be the opposite), typed on an old-fashioned machine in elite letters to fit a narrow strip of paper: OUT OF SIGHT & MIND, THERE IS A ROOM BY ALMOST ALL FORGOTTEN. WITHIN ITS WALLS LIES A SECRET OF THIS HOTEL NONE OF YOU WILL CARE TO KNOW. Wondering what it means, the Shepherdess brushes her kneecaps clean of imitation sand and packs the picnic hamper, though the cold chicken is scarcely touched. "Let's go," she says. "The Prime Minister may have the answer to this conundrum." Disappointed, I damn the bottle and its cryptic message, damn her and the P.M. both. "But I was having fun!" I grumble. "I'm reminded that there are other things in life besides it," she remonstrates. Upstairs on the mezzanine, the Prime Minister is playing backgammon with the General while the Conductor dozes over a foxed and yellowed score of Johann Strauss the Younger's, discovered by the Masseuse under a mattress in the Vienna Suite. (How it came to be there, no one knows as is the case in so much else concerning this hotel.) "We found a message in a bottle," the Shepherdess explains to justify our intrusion. The always imperturbable General screws in his monocle and smiles at what he sees—the girl, not me or the bottle! "Here it is, read it." The P.M. does and is nonplused: "What room and where?" With a debonaire wave of a liver-spotted hand, the General proposes that we look for it. The octogenarian Bell Captain (who, when a Bellboy, peeked into every room and closet) leads our anabasis. In the library, shelves endlessly replicate themselves, vanishing in the varnished distance like an exercise in forced perspective. "Why are so many empty?" the P.M. asks, having opened a dozen volumes. "They are those that have been forgotten," the Librarian says. "Each book erased by time, however, is replaced by another." And in her hands, we watch a white page darken as a photograph in the developer does. "This is the place to have my second childhood!" the General laughs, speeding away on a two-wheeled ladder hanging from a ceiling rail. In the Madame Tussaud

Room, where the Taxidermist spends his time, there are bins of parts belonging to every taxonomy including human. Pink swan necks loll in lazy SSSSS from a rack, waiting to replace those throttled out of boredom by the guests. We do not enter the world behind the next door (whose rumor makes us sqeamish) and visit, instead, the Charcot Room, drawn there by the noise of snoring. "*Shhh*!" the Analyst enjoins as we tiptoe in the dark. On beds half a dozen men and women are unconscious, wires fastened to their heads. "What's this?" we ask, surprised. "My Sleep Institute," he answers smugly. "The beds are occupied round the clock by dreamers." "So the hotel and everything that happens in it are dreamt by *them*?" we ask. The Analyst tugs his beard and mutters that he can't be sure. "But I would not risk annihilation by unplugging them!" We agree and leave without another word. On the topmost floor, there is a room where amanuenses type in shifts. "Of all the rooms we've seen so far, this one is the most bizarre!" exclaims the Shepherdess, straining to hear the tiny voices leaking from the Dictaphones. "There is a theory held by some that hotel life is fiction," says the Writer, who is shy and middle-aged. Anxiety seldom lets him mingle with the guests. "They dare not stop for fear the hotel will evaporate." "What do the voices say?" "They tell stories recorded on wax cylinders arriving each morning—who knows from where or by whom they're sent." We shudder to think existence might depend on typing and hurry from the room. There seems to be no end of rooms, and we look inside them all. At last, sandwiches eaten and flasks dry, we stumble into the hotel's dungeon whose rusty instruments would make Joan of Arc recant! Whether their purpose lies buried in the past or will be revealed in time is hidden from us. Afraid, we hurry up the stairs and dance (unaware that the tune the orchestra is playing is Lizst's *Totentanz*). On the balcony the Writer turns away and sees, beyond the hotel's walls, the engines of Malice waiting for us all.

40.

Death has entered the hotel and with it Realism. "We are afraid," we say one to another in the barroom where we have cloistered ourselves against violence and vulgarity. "We are fantasists," the Prime Minister observes, "and have no right to escape a dark age such as ours." Well read in the Moderns, the Barber counters thus: "We were once outside and could do nothing to stem the blood-red tide as Yeats called the anarchy then loose upon the world. I, for one, do not wish to drown unless it be for love in a Venetian canal, accompanied by an elegiac cello." Fond of rum, the Cellist begins to weep, saying: "Would I could be there when you do! But I am hydrophobic!" The Prime Minister, unconvinced by the Barber's glossing, rebukes him: "You hope in this way to extenuate your desertion of humanity, or is it from?" "Are we not also humanity, though a small and—by many—despiséd part?" the Barber orates with a rhetorical flourish reminding me of a spit-curl. I leave them to their wrangle, knowing the issue has no resolution. A Western Union Messenger steps smartly onto the stage. (This is theater after all!) "For you, sir," he says, handing me a blue telegram, which rustles pleasantly when I open it. I SHALL BE CROSSING THE ROTUNDA CEILING AT 8. WE MUST LEAVE THE HOTEL, NOW THAT IT IS NOT SO HOSPITABLE TO DREAMING. YOUR FUNAMBULIST. I arrive well before the appointed hour. One must be punctual for a tryst with someone who is never still. The Rotunda is dark. But through the windows that pierce it, night seeps, lightening the gloom. No longer willing to abet our insularity since the arrival of the floating dead, the Carpenter has unboarded the hotel's windows. In the morning the guests will confront day and day them, and their fancies will be dispelled like scraps of paper scattered by a wind-machine. "I'm here, Norman," the Funambulist whispers from her great height. (Whispers, nevertheless I hear!) "Hello, dear," I whisper in return, marveling at the dome's acoustic properties. "I'm ready to go with you, but where?" "To the moon," she answers. "It slipped its bonds inside the trolley barn while its abductors slept." And as if cued by her, a light slices through the windows that ring the mezzanine—dazzling and unbearable were it not coolly lunar. It powders the Funambulist's face and those of my friends standing like statues on the mezzanine, at the railing foiled in silver. "Come," says my Funambulist wife. I touch the dial of the watch given me by the Engineer, containing a tiny gyro and device patented by Count von Zeppelin. With it I have the lightness to ascend. I rise into the arms of my bride, saying *adieux* to the moonlit figures, which may or may not be real. Having no further need, she lets go her balancing-pole. It floats above the high-wire while— together—she and I go through the roof and on out into the night.

TO EACH
ACCORDING TO HIS
SENTENCE

Words create out of silence and
nothing everything we know.
—Alessandro Comi

1.

I have not read Gaston Leroux's 1908 novel *The Phantom of the Opera*. Like many others, I know the story by its cinematic adaptations: the 1925 silent film with Lon Chaney as the Phantom and the 1945 version starring Claude Rains. (There are newer treatments.) I do not wish to read the novel nor is reading it in any way essential to my purpose, which is to recreate *The Phantom of the Opera*. You will be led, inevitably, to think of Borges; but believe me, I am not such a fool as to attempt what he has done! In any case his intention, if it can ever be said to be known, is not mine. Mine is to build an edifice of prose in which to hide. What drink had done, words will now do. According to commentaries I have read, the 1925 film version is more faithful to the novel than the 1945 variant, although the former omits much of the original. Neither version contains what in the original is for me of principal interest: that the Phantom was an architect employed in the construction of the Opera's cellars. This detail in the Phantom's background suggested to me a possible way out of an increasingly impossible détente with—I leave it to you to say what.

My first impulse was to create anew, i.e., to write a story in which to achieve my end. I struggled for months, however, without discovering a narrative structure with a *mise en scène* so richly provided with hiding places as the Phantom's. (Not even in Borges do we find Leroux's gothic elaboration of the principle of concealment, perhaps because the Frenchman had, in aid of his imagination, the actual Paris Opera House.) At last I determined to follow the example of the hermit crab and borrow another's construction: Leroux's novel and its cinematic equivalents. I would appropriate the story as I knew it (a conflation of sources). Having found a form to inhabit, there remained the problem of how to insert myself into it.

2.

In the Phantom's rooms far below the Paris Opera, there are two mirrors: one in which the silvering behind the glass has tarnished, making all that is reflected in it obscure, and another that presents to each thing seen within it its likeness. At times the Phantom wishes to see himself as he is—in all his ugliness—and will gaze hours on end in the second mirror. For a while he will be a tragic figure, a Werther doomed to a life underground, despised, shunned—a castaway deprived of hope and love. He will revel in an austere pathos, making it his meat and drink—his tainted meat and bitter drink— until pathos, drained of tragic feeling, becomes maudlin. He will long then for the sentimentalities of song and beauty—that of a woman, young and virtuous, whose chaste lips taste of violet pastilles, a woman altogether worthy of his abasement. He will weep luxuriously. He will become drunk. He will submit himself to the engines and instruments of torture installed in the Opera's cellars during the Second Revolution. He will compose for the organ Romantic rhapsodies. At other times, however, the Phantom is impelled to gaze at himself in the tarnished mirror (the one the world calls kind). Touching his disfigured face, he becomes a grim Realist, who understands that what can be seen of the world is not in any case the truth. It is then he is most to be feared, for he will wish nothing more than to destroy beauty, to remove its pleasing mask—even with a knife.

THE PHANTOM: I have not left the Opera House since escaping Devil's Island [or overseeing the construction of the Opera's cellars, depending on one's source material] and taking refuge underground. But I go out on the roof at night when moved by the music and sit atop the statue of the winged figure above the frieze of grotesques.

3.

I was neither attracted to the Phantom's suffering (sumptuous though it may be) nor did I pity him his agony or the hell in which fate—say, rather, accident (of birth or engraver's acid) had consigned him. No, the solitariness of his life in the cellars of the Opera House drew me to his story—this, and his having been the architect of his own prison. That a man's search for privacy should have been abetted by a genius (however perverse) for form— this I, a writer dismayed by the presence of others, found attractive. How I came to this extremity of reserve I do not know. Whether by sudden contract with sobriety, made in a hospital emergency room, or the result of something less apocalyptic—all I do know is that I lacked a necessary defense against the world and could not— cannot—endure it.

THE PHANTOM: Consider what it means to have been shut away in a cell beneath the Opera House—there to be subjected to torments unknown even by the damned, whose chief desire is to die. Like them to pray daily to be dead and to curse God at finding oneself yet alive; to say endless rosaries of suffering and to endure savage martyrdoms; to undergo incomparable mortifications and to invent anew the theorems of annihilation and remain, in spite of all, caged inside one's own hated self—hated because it insists on sovereignty over death and will not, will not even in hell's fifth cellar, let go of life! Think further of this same animal (for he cannot be said any longer to be a man) cornered by walls, which to gnaw on is to break even rats' teeth, released into the open air at last only to be delivered into another hell—a flowery, tropical vacation hell where all that is rots and rot is all there is. They set me down among lepers and the mad and would have fed my corpse to shark or crocodile or the accommodating mire! Devil's Island. No place more aptly named! No place in the history of torment better equipped to hollow out a man and fill the cavity with gall! Having suffered this (you cannot know all that "this" entails) and having borne it, or not borne it, accompanied by such a disfigurement as mine—do you wonder I am cruel, that I can be moved swiftly to murder? Wonder, instead, how I could not be otherwise. I ought to be dead, wanting nothing else; but denied that balm and deliverance, I am and can be no other than a malignant rage.

Unlike the Phantom, I am not disfigured, deformed, or solitary. At least in none of the visible dimensions. I am of ordinary appearance and possessed of a wife, two grown children, and a sufficiency of friends (meaning enough to appease a small appetite for society but not so many as to make writing impossible). I am, as I said, embarrassed by the presence of others outside that little circle of intimate relations; racked by self-consciousness; encumbered by the obligation to converse with strangers so as not to be considered strange. The truth is I wish to be thought of not at all—neither looked at, discussed, nor weighed and found wanting. I wish to be invisible like him, like the Phantom, and to be left alone to do my work. We are creative men, whose joy is only in creation; both bedeviled by an unopposable need to invent forms. His genius was to have designed a structure (the labyrinthine cellars beneath the Opera House) that concealed him and modeled his unconscious mind. (If the mollusk has a mind, might not its thoughts be deduced from the topology of its shell?) My intention in these pages is to follow the Phantom's example (and also, perhaps, the mollusk's): to devise a form in which I can disappear.

THE PHANTOM: I might have been content to remain as I am, where I am, if it were not for ambition, which gnaws me, and love in which I burn—skin, hair on fire, eyes scalded, a human torch not to be put out even in death. I might have been content to be master of all I survey, lord of the underworld, making a royal progress daily through the five cellars of hell, whose rooms and passages multiply in a lunatic arithmetic beyond the knowledge of their architect. There are worse than I put away, deformities greater than mine shut up in more grievous confinement than this. I tell you I would have been content—more than content—happy!—to have found myself in this meager granary provided, nevertheless, with enough to nourish dreaming. Does a rat not dream even of its sewer, and is not the sewer, being all there is, not a sufficient condition for a rat's happiness? Or have you never given thought to a rat—you in your wider, sunnier world? The companionable rats dream as do I—of walls of brick, stone, and earth, of the black lake that laps the foundations of the Paris Opera House and makes a not unmusical sound in the sluices like the flushing all at once of a thousand water-closets. And do you think that rats do not apprehend music of a mineral modality, whose timbre is an oozing and whose dynamic *sotto voce*? I have seen them transfixed by sounds at audition's furthermost limit, like Elijah in his cave by the voice of the Almighty. And if a rat can be so enthralled, how much, then, the man who hears for the first time an angelic voice? And if that man is I and the voice that of Christine Daaé—how can I do otherwise than burn?

4.

Charles Garnier designed the visible Opéra National de Paris. By visible I mean that which can be observed either above the street or below it. The Phantom's engagement with the complex structure is illusory. Allow me to retract: the Phantom's design for the tortuous cellars beneath the 15,000-square-meter building is real insofar as it was conceived in the imagination of Gaston Leroux, author of *The Phantom of the Opera* and of its malevolent central figure. To say that Garnier's subterranean construction is "more real" (or less) than Leroux's (or the Phantom's) is to become embroiled in a philosophical controversy for which I am not trained. (Leroux's Opera House does stand and impresses us greatly.) I am equally unwilling to conduct a stale inquiry into fiction as a valid model—

or even a substitute for—the verifiable realm of fact. Suffice it to say that Garnier created his Opera House in a traditional Italian style inspired by the Grand Theatre in Bordeaux, built by Victor Louis in 1870, and by the Italian and French villas of the seventeenth and eighteenth centuries. Leroux's was influenced by Garnier's, and the Phantom's cellars by the topology of his own imagination, his disfigurement, or both.

Two events (one geological, the other political) impeded the building's construction: discovery of a lake far below the building site and the 1870 Franco-Prussian War, with the ensuing siege and reduction of the Paris Commune. The latter not only halted construction but resulted in the Phantom's incarceration in the fifth cellar. Time emptied the dungeons of their prisoners and rid them of the tangible apparatus of torture. (They continued in the Phantom's mind.) Engineering raised a massive concrete well to carry the Opera's immense stage and fly-tower and flooded the well to counter the pressure of the underground lake. (Thus, overcoming the geological impediment.) The Black Lake as it is called by Leroux, on which the Opera's stage can be said to "float," is—for me—the novel's principal topographical feature. Indeed, my interest in the Opera House's architecture centers not on Garnier's grandiose achievement above ground but on the Phantom's cellars (or Leroux's if you insist on making the usual distinction between a novelist and his character. Both men having been architects of an identical space, I do not—in this case—make the distinction). In fact my optimism concerning my relocation to the cellars lies here: if Leroux could build his underground out of nothing but words and attribute its design to his character the

Phantom—I, too, can build the cellar in my own century and with my own words, out of my own nothing. And in building it, I will become—like the Phantom—a character inside it.

THE PHANTOM: Lately I feel the presence of an interloper. At first I believed it was the Persian, who lurks in the Opera's dim corners to spy on me. Or Christine's lover, Raoul, or his brother, Philippe, the Comte de Chagny. Or the secret policeman—or someone employed by the Opera's managers after I had purloined their wine and left them my ultimatum regarding Christine and the fate of La Carlotta, should she fail to yield to her young rival the role of Margarita. If my threats are not taken seriously, let the catastrophe be on their heads! How can they fail to prefer Christine, whose reach, tone, clarity, and declamatory power are superior to Carlotta's? Who better than I can judge her absolute authority of voice? Not these vermin! Christine is an object of constant obsession. The *desideratum*. My devotion to her voice, her career, and to her sweet self is single-minded. And yet ... something there is that gets into my mind of late— interfering and disturbing. The voice of a man—not sweet, not melodious, not even French—whose quality is a querulousness I consider inane. What is his tribulation against my own? I feel him hunting the margins of my story, probing for a way inside.

5.

From his apartments in the fifth cellar, the Phantom can enter, by means of subterranean ways and secret passages, rooms in the Opera House itself. He comes and goes, freely and undetected, through panels cunningly concealed in the wainscoting, trapdoors, and the full-length mirrors in the performers' dressing-rooms. He persuades Christine Daaé to follow him below by passing from her room's mirror to one of the two mirrors in his. (I am inclined toward Professor Lishkovitz's view that the passage is psychical and that the mirror in which the Phantom gazes—and draws Christine to himself by his gaze—will determine whether he appears to her as a sentimental lover enamored of her voice or as a homicidal maniac incited by desire.)

Yesterday, my therapist wondered—provocatively—if I could be content, hiding within an "edifice of prose," were I no longer able to write and, should I be able, to what degree my happiness depends on publishing the results. I must admit that my happiness is dependent on both conditions being met and am optimistic that a way will be found for me to do both, as a fiction within a fiction. One can write anywhere! Publishing is, of course, problematic. Within all but the most scrupulously objective narratives, however, there is a general telepathy; my hope is that I can use it to "send" my work out into the world. I will look to the Phantom for whatever technical facilities may be required. He will not deny me what services he is, by nature, equipped to provide!

A fiction within a fiction? Surely I can be nothing else, once ensconced inside the Phantom's story! Unless being conscious of my self (of my being Norman Lock) is sufficient to satisfy actuality's minimum requirement; in which case I will be an actual presence inside Leroux's own edifice of prose. (In what way and to what degree I may alter Leroux's original structure by the "spaciousness" of an existence no matter how seemingly cramped, I leave to Post-Structuralists.) I assume—I can do nothing else!—that I will receive by the grace and power of the imagination (the Phantom's or those who will subsequently encounter me in reading or by other mechanical means) raiment—that is to say, flesh or flesh's simulacrum. I shall not be a ghost. Whether I will, in time, be bewitched by Christine (if we do indeed come to inhabit the same story), whether or not I will, like Erik, love her and, unlike him, consummate that love— all this remains to be seen. I do believe that the present inadequacies of my personality will vanish when I have disappeared inside *The Phantom of the Opera*.

THE PHANTOM: Ambition, too, goads me. The gala when Christine, as Margarita, swept La Carlotta into the dust-bin, in the prison scene and final trio of *Faust*— that night Gounod conducted his *Funeral March of a Marionette*, Reyer his Overture to *Siguar*, Massenet a Hungarian march, Guiraud his *Carnaval*, Saint Saens the *Danse Macabre* and a *Reverie Orientale*. I ought to have been among them, smirking at the mob as it surged forward on the ballet foyer! If I were not ... unprepossessing. Ha! I exceed all definitions of ugliness! Quasimodo's is nothing next to mine. Esmeralda would not have given *me* water. I am grotesque like the Opera gargoyles in whose company I indulge in nocturnal rages at the City of Light. I am more animal than man, more mineral than animal—scoria, slag of the Beast's foundry, lava of Vesuvius, cinder of a burnt offering. To see me is to be turned to salt, to stone—is to gain admission in an instant to Charenton Asylum—is to be struck deaf, dumb, and blind. God knows I am repulsive! But if I were not, my genius would be proclaimed, my music famous, my face adored. I would be illustrious, and Christine would not have swooned at the sight of me.

6.

To enter Leroux's edifice, I must first become prose. Only as words can matter and its energy exist among other words. I sometimes think that when the last word is spoken or set down—at the moment utterance ceases— all that is will vanish, will become again the aboriginal thought. The film will run in reverse through recorded and unrecorded time all the way back to Nothing. (I believe that a case can be made for everything that is as being only words—knowable by words, invoked by words, and created by them. But I will not make it here.) And when I have entered *The Phantom of the Opera*, will I—like Wells's Martian machines, perish by a germ endemic to melodrama or will I—a foreign body—carry off the Phantom?

The fifth cellar incorporates the principal features of an eighteenth-century pleasure park. There are a room of mirrors, a chamber of horrors, a maze, and boats moving silently through a flooded grotto. None was in Garnier's original plan or in Leroux's projection of it onto the fictional space of *The Phantom of the Opera*. These are elaborations made by the Phantom, who as a child was captivated by holiday visits to the Tivoli Gardens in Copenhagen and the Prater in Vienna. (Theories of the novel aside, you must grant me that a character will sometimes take on a life of its own, seemingly independent of its author's conception. What else can we mean when, in the presence of remarkable fiction, we say that a character lives and continues to do so after we have closed the book on its recounted history? And to live is to change, at least subtly, the surrounding world.) Reminded of my own novel *The Long Rowing unto Morning*, I thought that, in the submerged channels spreading like black lace beneath the Opera House, I might insert myself—as prose—into Leroux's novel and the Phantom's actualization of it. I have already constructed—in words—an eminently stable and watertight boat and demonstrated—in words—that I know how to set it going. I will, then, row my way inside the edifice! It requires only a single sentence, ostensibly written by Leroux (and rendered into English)—perhaps in an early draft of his novel, suppressed or forgotten until now: *The oar blades dipped and rose, scattering garnets and rubies in profusion in the fitful light of flambeaux which, at regular intervals, relieved the grotto's otherwise absolute dark, as M. Lock entered the Black Lake.*

THE PHANTOM: The intuition that a person extraneous, adventitious, alien to my world has been probing the margin for a way inside is now a certainty. He has come by boat: I have heard the oarlocks creak in the brick vaults and the rats' alarms. I am used to intruders and know how to scare them off. Those that won't scare, I murder. As architect of the *mise en scène*, the advantage is always mine. But against this infiltrator, I have none; he knows what I know—every secret passage, trapdoor, and sluice. If all that I know can be told in words, he has imagined them. If every brick is a word and every drape in whose folds I can hide is, too—those words are also his. I am bound to him and he to me by a paradigm established elsewhere. Call it my sentence. My only hope to escape it is to act arbitrarily. Only in the principle by which rooms and corridors propagate and mirrors unfold unplotted spaces can I be free of an invisible dependency. The Persian, Raoul, Philippe, the secret policeman, the Opera's managers and minions—they want to put an end to my incursions into the upper world from which I am banished. They want to be rid of me as you would a rat. I understand them—their repugnance. But this other who inserts himself into my realm—what can he want? Certainly he does not mean to befriend me, obtain for me justice, or restore me to the podiums of the great orchestras of Europe. He can have come only to harm me, kill me, expel me from the only place in which I exist: this story, these words of Gaston Leroux's, surrounding and defining me, which I enlarge according to my capacity and will. Do not ask how I know! I do as the sluice does the pressure of water or the lightning-rod the electric current's heat. I know it the way an actor would if something not written were introduced into the play. My antagonist is rowing upon the Black Lake. I might release the pent water that acts as counter-pressure to the lake on which the stage floats; it would be a second Deluge. Would he drown in his boat, or has he foreseen my hands on the massive valves? I ought to put on my cloak and hurry into the passages to seek in the Opera's foundations that part built according to an irrational design. If I could chance upon a moment of expansion when time stretches like an elastic, the cramped view enlarges to a panorama, the space between atoms yawns—if I could only! But I am weary suddenly of the game in which I have been made to play. Leroux! It would have been better had I been left ignorant of my author; better yet if I had never been. I wish you had been run down by a carriage, carried off by fever, or had written instead about the man in the moon! I feel the other's presence like a microbe and am made sick to death! I will not join the rats tumbling pell-mell over the Turkish carpet. I will play Bach—*Passacaglia and Fugue*—and wait.

7.

I tie the boat to a heavy ring and climb stone stairs slippery with ooze. Light from a pair of smoking torches trembles on the black water. The air is foul. A rat climbs over another, then falls into the sluice. On the other side of the iron door, the Phantom plays Bach's *Passacaglia and Fugue*. The playing is manic, portentous, doom-cadenced; and I am aware suddenly of what I risk by my intercalation—the danger in hoping to lose myself in another's story. But my abnegation has been thorough; already I have acquired something of a character's insubstantiality. The Phantom has his cloak, his mask, and his scars with which to imprint another's memory, while my face in its bland ordinariness has nothing to commend it. I had intended to keep out of his way, haunting the Opera House's labyrinthine passages, listening to music and silence. But the story's magnetism drew me at once to its center. The boat fetched up at the Phantom's door.

Anna Karenina, Marguerite Gautier, Lear, Kurtz— what was death for them? Is there pain in the words of pain's depiction? Is death no more than an end to words? If I should, while writing this sentence, stop, never to begin again, is that death? When the Phantom kills me (he must, for there is room only for a single tragic destiny in Leroux's conception), will I become the word *corpse*, left to lie where it fell upon the page like cigar ash, which the reader in his headlong flight will forget? Or will I simply enter the white space where writing does not exist? And is this not what I wanted?

THE PHANTOM: By a moment's inattention, I may unbind myself from the one on the other side of the door, from Leroux's nightmare, from the rack of my special destiny. It needs only art—a momentary bending of its rigor. If in the twentieth and final variation I transpose certain of the notes or depart briefly the key signature or linger overlong on the pedal, it will be enough, perhaps, to disenthrall me. By error I may escape my assassin and the mob whose own destiny it is to harry me tonight into the Seine! I may escape, as well, Christine, who is bound to the bed of my desire by Leroux's rope and whose mouth is muted with his handkerchief. I will rise from the organ, which will have ceased intoning another's music, put on my cloak and hat, and walk out of the Opera House into a soft Parisian night—handsome and free of the thralldom of art. And should a reader turn anew to Leroux's story, it will not be I buried beneath the Opera House but another delivered up according to his sentence.

I sometimes think that when the last word is spoken or set down—at the moment utterance ceases—all that is will vanish ...

NORMAN LOCK has written novels and short fiction as well as stage, radio and screen plays. He received the 1979 Aga Kahn Prize, given by *The Paris Review*. He is a recipient of fellowships from the New Jersey Council on the Arts and from the Pennsylvania Council on the Arts—both for fiction—and, in 2011, for poetry from the National Endowment for the Arts. His latest prose works are the novels *Shadowplay* and *The King of* Sweden, published by Ellipsis Press and Ravenna Press, respectively, and the short-fiction collection *Grim Tales*, released this year in a new version by Mud Luscious Press. *Shadowplay* received the 2010 literary fiction prize, given by The Dactyl Foundation. Norman lives in Aberdeen, New Jersey, with his wife, Helen.

S P U Y T E N   D U Y V I L
Meeting Eyes Bindery
Triton

Inverted Curvatures   Francis Raven

Jackpot   Tsipi Keller

The Jazzer & The Loitering Lady   Gordon Osing

Knowledge   Michael Heller

Lady V.   D.R. Popa

Last Supper of the Senses   Dean Kostos

A Lesser Day   Andrea Scrima

Let's Talk About Death   M. Maurice Abitbol

Light House   Brian Lucas

*Light Years: Multimedia in the East
                    Village, 1960-1966*   (ed.) Carol Bergé

Little Book of Days   Nona Caspers

Little Tales of Family & War   Martha King

Long Fall: Essays and Texts   Andrey Gritsman

Lunacies   Ruxandra Cesereanu

Lust Series   Stephanie Dickinson

Lyrical Interference   Norman Finkelstein

Maine Book   Joe Cardarelli (ed. Anselm Hollo)

Mannhatten   Sarah Rosenthal

Medieval Ohio   Richard Blevins

Memory's Wake   Derek Owens

Mermaid's Purse   Laynie Browne

Mobility Lounge   David Lincoln

The Moscoviad   Yuri Andrukhovych

Multifesto: A Henri d'Mescan Reader   Davis Schneiderman

No Perfect Words   Nava Renek

No Wrong Notes   Norman Weinstein

North & South   Martha King

Notes of a Nude Model   Harriet Sohmers Zwerling

Of All The Corners To Forget   Gian Lombardo

Our Father   M.G. Stephens